PENGUIN
SPECIALS

Penguin Specials fill a gap. Written by some of today's most exciting and insightful writers, they are short enough to be read in a single sitting – when you're stuck on a train; in your lunch hour; between dinner and bedtime. Specials can provide a thought-provoking opinion, a primer to bring you up to date, or a striking piece of fiction. They are concise, original and affordable.

To browse digital and print Penguin Specials titles, please refer to **www.penguin.com.au/penguinspecials**

T0165676

Professor Su Jing'an in His Later Years

by

DONG JUN

A Novella

Translated from the original
Chinese by Sid Gulinck

PENGUIN BOOKS

UK | USA | Canada | Ireland | Australia
India | New Zealand | South Africa | China

Penguin Books is part of the Penguin Random House group of companies
whose addresses can be found at global.penguinrandomhouse.com

Penguin
Random House
PENGUIN BOOKS

This paperback edition published by Penguin Group (Australia), 2019

13 5 7 9 10 8 6 4 2

Text copyright © Dong Jun, 2019

Translated from the Chinese by Sid Gulinck

Produced with Writers Association of Zhejiang Province
Originally published in Chinese as *Su Jing'an Jiaoshou Wannian Tanhua Lu*
with the Writers Association of Zhejiang Province

The moral right of the author has been asserted.

Cover design by Di Suo © Penguin Group (Australia)
Text design by Steffan Leyshon-Jones © Penguin Group (Australia)
Printed and bound in China by RR Donnelley Asia Printing Solutions Ltd.

ISBN: 9780734398673

penguin.com.au

MIX
Paper from
responsible sources
FSC
www.fsc.org   FSC™ C144853

About the Translator

Sid Gulinck is a Belgian sinologist and certified interpreter who has spent over a decade researching Chinese language and culture. Currently based in the northern Chinese city of Tianjin, he specializes in translation and interpreting with a focus on the Chinese cultural, literary and artistic fields.

Professor Su Jing'an in His Later Years

The call from our Centre Director, unexpected as it was, came as I was browsing for books in a quaint little second-hand book shop near Jing'an temple. It was a Sunday afternoon in early spring of last year. After flipping shut the cell phone, I closed my eyes, and was so thrilled I had to keep myself from blurting out insults. From the moment I answered that call, I became vaguely aware of the foreseeable turn my life would take. This call didn't get me promoted at the research institute, nor bumped up to a higher pay grade for that matter. Those were things I had never cared for to begin with. The thing that exhilarated me so was of another nature, something a bibliophile like myself could only happen upon per chance, rather than by design. After I returned home, I was barely able to conceal my enthusiasm, so I made myself a cup of green tea, turned on the computer, and wrote the following abstruse sentence on my personal blog:

'Jing'an temple. Professor Su Jing'an. What unequivocal link connects the two?'

The following morning, I called the number given to me by our Centre Director and got in touch with Professor Su Jing'an, that Master of Chinese Studies, whom I had admired so much. Now that he had retired, he consented to me becoming his caretaker, a task designated to me by the centre which I accepted with glee. As a matter of fact, my literary affinity with Professor Su ran deep. I first started reading his books back in college. Once, after finding out he was to deliver a lecture about the history of ancient Chinese fables at the Faculty of Historical Studies, I frenziedly rushed to the venue to attend the lecture with a couple of his acclaimed books in hand. At the time, Su Jing'an was still in his early sixties, sporting a hairdo interspersed with greying locks, dressed in a classically tasteful and neatly tailored blue shirt. He set the tone for his lecture by saying the following: 'Everyone go ahead and make yourselves at home. First of all, feel free to smoke in class, for yours truly is a passionate smoker. Second, go ahead and leave mid-class if you so please, or take a nap, which I'll take as a sign that my lectures are dull, seeing how you don't want to lend me your ears. Third, I'll leave fifteen minutes at the end of the class for questions or rebuttals.'

Professor Su's class was packed to the brim, and

laughter and applause resounded from beginning to end. He gave the impression of being rigid yet witty, restrained yet untrammeled. I recall drawing a caricature of him in his lecture that day; in the picture, I did my best to highlight his oversized spectacles, a fuming tongue and a cigar for a finger. Professor Su's books have accompanied me all this time, and with each rereading, they've provided me with new insights. Whenever he published a new book, I would buy it and place it by the side of my bed. Rather than finishing it in one go, I would give it a cursory browse so I had something to look forward to the next day.

Late last year, I read an article by a renowned historian, published in a prestigious academic journal. After exposing the author's haphazard guesswork concerning a lesser known ancient Chinese character, I instantly wrote a 2000 character-long exposé on the character in question. I emailed my piece to the journal's editor, who ended up reprinting it word for word. It was met with moderate response but prompted a few scholars to approach me via email to discuss some weighty issues. As a matter of fact, I merely happened to know an arcane Chinese character unknown to most other people,which weirdly enough helped garner me the title of Senior Scholar. I felt somewhat abashed about the whole ordeal. After stumbling upon my essay, our Centre Director came to me in high spirits and we spent the afternoon discussing that one-of-a-kind ancient character. During our conversation, I admitted to being indebted to an old publication of Su Jing'an's for this academic find of mine. At the height of our exchange, I even showed him one of my essays on the writings of Su Jing'an.

'Long ago, upon graduating, way before my time', our Director said reminiscently while twirling a pencil around in his hand, 'Su Jing'an was assigned to my current position. He was quite the eccentric. There was a period when he'd bring a fruit knife on dates with his sweetheart. Later on, he'd often come into work with a calculus textbook. It was obvious he never had a use for that knife nor textbook, but he enjoyed filling his cloth tote bag with arbitrary items.'

The numerous anecdotes our Centre Director shared with me kindled my interest in Professor Su Jing'an's private life. Little did I know our Centre Director would end up putting me in touch with Su Jing'an, and even procure for me this gratifying assignment. As a caretaker to Professor Su Jing'an, I'd be on the payroll at my work unit, while also being able to make academic inquiries. I would truly be killing two birds with one stone. Previously, nothing had been more of a nuisance than dealing with trifling matters at work. During business trips, people always called on me, making it impossible for me to loaf around on the job even if I tried. It felt like I was living for them instead of for myself. This was now all in the past, and I could finally cast off those suffocating trifles like a pair of worn trainers.

The next morning, I arrived an hour early at Professor's estate, dubbed the Bamboo and Plum Blossom Pavilion. He and his wife each sat at a corner of the table, reading the paper over breakfast. Professor Su had the housekeeper usher me into the study, where I was to wait a while. The study was bigger than I'd imagined. Many of the books on the shelves had on blue cloth sleeves, making them appear extremely precious. Aside from the books, another thing that drew me in was the varied collection of clocks in the room, all of which ran differently; some ran a little early, others a little late. Only one of the clocks ran in sync with my own watch, its dials displaying that it was five past eight. Upon careful inspection I could make out the tiny lettering at the bottom of each one, which read 'Paris time', 'Berlin time', 'Rome time', 'Tokyo time', 'New York time', 'Prague time', 'Athens time', 'Lisbon time', 'Amsterdam time', 'Madrid time', 'London time', 'Vienna time' and 'Buenos Aires time'. All cities which, if I recall correctly, were featured in a travel journal Professor Su had recently published. In the preface to the book, he wrote as follows: 'All in this world converges wherever there are books.'

Su Jing'an's study was different than others, in that it exuded a strong and distinct personal sensibility. Surrounded by the international times displayed on each of the clocks, the world map on the wall and the vast collection of foreign language books, you felt like this man was living at the centre of the earth. Up-close perusal transported you to the far corners of the globe: you could cross the European continent just by lifting a leg and touch the fountainhead of the ancient Greek civilization by extending your hand. As I was leafing through a book, Professor Su walked in. Having asked me about some personal details, he blew out a whiff of smoke and said, 'I've read some of your articles, they're quite good. But don't get carried away just yet.' I quickly nodded in affirmation.

Mrs Su, who came in a bit later carrying fruit, seemed polite and considerate. More than twenty years his junior, she was nearing fifty, and was in possession of that tranquil beauty which had once moved a poet to wax lyrical, calling it 'porcelain-like'. Sitting in front of me, Mrs Su looked like a model you see in those old sepia portrait photographs. The streaks of pale yellow light falling in through the drapes gave the room an almost chiaroscuro quality, which was permeated with the beguiling, bitter aroma of morning coffee. You could virtually smell the incoming sunlight.

Mrs Su had been a postgrad student of Professor

Su's. Under his guidance, she'd translated poems by such poets as Mallarmé and Baudelaire. It was thus only natural that our conversation gravitated towards French poetry. Mrs Su said that since getting married to Professor Su over twenty years ago, she hadn't read any French poetry, let alone discussed the likes of Baudelaire. These days, though, her conversations tended to centre on her mahjong manual book. Mrs Su was a prolific mahjong player, and she'd risen to fame amongst the wives of college professors for her proficiency at shuffling the tiles. Professor Su waved off our mahjong chat and told his wife to 'go and attend to her tiles then.' She rolled her eyes at him and left the room.

Professor Su handed me a new book, and said contemptuously, 'This pupil of Wang Zhiyong's, he's truly beyond cure. He misinterpreted a perfectly good essay.'

His excitement could be inferred from the excess saliva forming at the corners of his mouth, which he quickly licked off with his tongue. Professor Su gave me the original so I could compare and asked me to annotate one of the article's paragraphs. I was aware he did this to gauge my academic ability, which intimidated me somewhat. Modern day improvements in book printing have made horizontal page-setting and simplified characters look pleasing to the eye and all imperfections visible at a glance. But ancient books look so incredibly opaque, with their vertical mise-en-page, traditional characters and lack of punctuation.

After annotating and proofreading the passage, I handed the text back to Professor Su with trepidation. He read the whole thing and nodded approvingly, then very calmly pointed out a mistake. I took this opportunity to muster up the courage and ask the Professor forthrightly wether he and Professor Wang Zhiyong had worked together in the early days of our research centre, ending in their falling out over differences concerning a philosophical issue.

Professor Su didn't give me a straight answer, but pointed to the clock on the wall, saying 'It's as simple as this: a clock accurately tells us the time, but sometimes two clocks don't tell us the same accurate time. The dials of the clock in front of me point to Tokyo time, while yet another clock's dials point to Paris time.'

Professor Su was far more spirited of a man than Professor Wang Zhiyong. The two were about the same age and had both passed the seventy mark, but Professor Su likened his own old age to 'a good tune played on an old fiddle', and that of Professor Wang to plain old 'senility'. As he made this claim, his face revealed his old, boyish self. Professor Su continued the comparison, saying that at the beginning of the year, Wang Zhiyong had made several motions to retire due to health reasons, whilst he himself had brought up retirement on account of having to 'write several important treatises, as a legacy to later generations.'

He, therefore, felt Wang Zhiyong's retirement was incomparable to his own. Professor Su said, 'Some think of retirement as life ending, but for me, it's merely the beginning of another stage in life.'

He didn't condone spending one's old age alone, seated in some drab little corner, sunbathing and breathing comfortably. Either that or sitting in an old people's home with a bunch of retirees, playing some rounds of mahjong or finishing off a few games of Go. After all, Professor Su wouldn't be his usual self were he not beaming with energy and looking alive with ambition.

We then got down to business, and the Professor handed me his work plan. I leafed through it and couldn't contain my astonishment. 'I'm still only seventy-four,' Professor Su said, 'so I can spend five or six years on teasing out the Thirteen Classics and the Twenty-Four Histories. Then, when I get to eighty, I'll spend a decade writing a book on the history of Chinese thought. When I reach ninety, I'll take up my pen again to start work on my memoirs.'

According to his calculations, Professor Su would have had to live to at least a hundred, unhindered by illness. Judging from this work plan, I could tell that Professor Su had divided his time into several large segments, counted in years. These were then further divided in a number of smaller segments, made up of months. Those, in turn, were divided into days. Each day consisted of fixed time elements: morning exercise, siesta, afternoon tea, the making of blue cloth book sleeves. The remaining chunks of time were occupied by reading and writing. At four in the afternoon, meaning 5 p.m. Tokyo time, or 10 a.m. Paris time, Professor Su put down the book in his hands, turned off the desk lamp, retreated into the kitchen and came back with a pot of freshly brewed coffee. He made two cups and presented one to me. Half an hour later, the Professor got back to work; his inner mind was akin to a robust framework which enclosed scattered objects and subjected them to his own set of rules.

Why, indeed, Professor Su was quite anal about his rules for living. Each new day would start and end in more or less the same way as the last. It began with a pot of coffee and ended with a glass of milk. He seemed hard-pressed to change his way of life, and yet after his retirement, subtle changes had begun to occur. The first thing that had changed was his route. He used to always take subway line number four, then transfer to line three on his way to school to give lectures, and come back via the same route. Now that he was retired and at home, these two subway lines were no longer permanent fixtures in his life. He wasn't used to it at first, so he'd walk to the subway station and feel his pockets only to realise he didn't have his subway card on him and didn't need to show up for work anymore. To assuage this sense of unease, Professor Su went out for walks after sunrise every morning. 'In the first half of my life,' he said, 'my two hands brought me the joy of writing. Now, in the latter half of my life, my two feet bring me the joy of walking.'

The Professor's way of walking was different from other people's. He walked backwards, which made it look as if he was learning to walk from scratch. Several years earlier, the Professor had been the type of person who 'demanded ideological progress', whereas he was now well-versed in all things to do with the prefix '-re'. Retirement. Walking in reverse. Receding from an argument. Retreating under enemy fire, and responding to the enemy's retreat with a counterattack. Or even reciting the works of famed Tang-dynasty poet Han Yu. . .

Professor Su now spent more time walking backwards than he did moving forward. As soon as he exited that Bamboo and Plum Blossom Pavilion of his, he began walking backwards from Bamboo Grove Street, going past the concert hall, the science and technology museum, the Children's Palace, all the way to the big square, and then returned along the same path. The whole process was like a video recording in rewind. After walking back in a perfectly straight line, still maintaining his backward gait, the clock would strike seven as soon as he entered the house. I asked Professor Su why he enjoyed walking backwards, to which he replied wittily, 'With death looming ahead, all I can do is turn around and look back on the first half of my life.'

On the weekend, at nightfall, one of his fellow professors' wives called, wanting to convene with Professor Su's wife to try out a new restaurant, followed by an all-nighter of mahjong as per usual. Since the housekeeper, Xiao Wu, had already prepared dinner for both of them, and it would be a waste to chuck it, Professor Su invited me to dine with him. When I entered the kitchen to fill my plate, I caught a glimpse of a gleaming kitchen knife stuck in a cutting board. I wanted to pull it out, but Xiao Wu held me back. She whispered to me that Mrs Su always drove a kitchen knife in the cutting board before heading out to play mahjong. I didn't get the connection between racking up mahjong tiles and planting down a kitchen knife, and didn't deem it appropriate to pry into it further.

The table was filled with uniformly coloured vegetable dishes. From his books, I had gathered early on that Professor Su was a vegetarian. He asked me whether I could get used to a vegetarian diet and I replied that being treated to such a delectable spread of vegetable dishes was equivalent to getting the red-carpet treatment. Pleased to hear this, Professor Su kept on eating

12

as he explained to me the benefits of vegetarianism. Most vegetarians are even-tempered, and the same went for Professor Su. He said that a vegetarian diet helped fertilise the 'verdant mind', and could thus be beneficial for one's wisdom. In passing, I asked him whether his wife was also a vegetarian, to which he replied 'I'm not a Buddhist, but am a habitual vegetarian. My wife, on the other hand, is a Buddhist but eats meat. She'll only eat vegetarian dishes on the first or fifteenth day of the Lunar New Year, or as we say in the countryside, she's a fair-weather faster.'

He then pointed to a dish of salty sprouts and fermented bean curd, saying 'These two things are my must-haves with every meal. After I turned seventy, my palate became more and more like my father's.' Professor Su's old man had been a vegetable farmer in the countryside.

After Professor Su was done talking about his relatives, he began to praise his housekeeper Xiao Wu, who he said wasn't that well-educated, but was clever and hands-on nonetheless. As he taught her how to cook vegetarian dishes she had also proven herself to be a quick learner. When I asked Xiao Wu what skills were needed to prepare veggie dishes, she evaded the question, seemingly convinced that kitchen help wasn't the most lustrous of professions. Instead, she preferred to discuss current events she'd read about in the papers.

After finishing a modest serving of alcohol, Professor Su went into his study slightly tipsy and shut the door. Xiao Wu informed me that he'd gone back to making his blue book sleeves. I had seen those blue book sleeves, every one of which looked rugged and jagged. I asked Xiao Wu whether it'd be okay if I went and had a look, to which she replied that wasn't an option. While crafting his book sleeves, Professor Su was like a village tailor who kept his door shut out of fear of others picking up on his craft. I laughed and said it wasn't abnormal, what with the master losing his means of subsistence once his disciples had left his tutelage.

Xiao Wu held one chopstick upright and asked if I could teach her how to write poetry. I told her I only knew how to read poems, not write them. She let out a faintly audible 'Oh. . . ', then sighed and said how wonderful it must be to possess knowledge, to sit in a room every day, reading and writing, not needing to worry about the price of vegetables. As she said this, her glance revealed an adoration for knowledge. In more unequivocal terms, she adored the personification of knowledge, meaning Professor Su himself. She said that by spending time with him, she had picked up on a great deal of it herself. Hence, she preferred staying 'in the servitude of Professor Su, instead of at the head of a herd of livestock back in the countryside.'

I had no intention of prying into Professor Su's private life, yet each time Xiao Wu appeared before me, I couldn't help but venture a guess. I noticed that Xiao Wu did her best to look different. Her appearance was that of someone from an intellectual household. When not busy mopping the floor, or trimming vegetables, she sometimes consulted Professor Su about strange and intriguing inquiries. She also had an extraordinary ability to grasp the everyday, watered down snippets of knowledge found on the internet and television. She would share this 'knowledge' profusely, as a counterbalance to the pakchoi and the mop to which she routinely clung. This made me feel like she wasn't your run-of-the-mill country bumpkin, but rather a remarkable girl who expressed herself in remarkable ways. Gradually, it dawned on me that she, wittingly or not, was comparing herself to Mrs Su. She imitated the way Mrs Su took drags from her cigarette and even assumed her languid, heavy-hearted demeanour. Sometimes, a spell of light rain could cause her to lie on the couch dejectedly, or to suffer silently in a corner of the kitchen. At other times, in a bout of excitement, she put on Mrs Su's well-worn cheongsam, and slumped listlessly against the kitchen doorframe, then abruptly let out an artistically sounding quote from an ancient poem. Professor Su let me know that these mannerisms were in fact instilled in her by Mrs Su. I couldn't quite comprehend why Mrs Su would trade in the pleasures of a leisurely life to condition a country girl into becoming a 'literary youth', even thoroughly altering her aesthetic taste. In our breezy, upbeat conversations, she told me she'd discovered a sudden fondness for the wrinkles on old men's faces, which she treated like maxims of great profundity.

*

One Sunday morning, Professor Su called me up to say some of his favourite pupils had arranged to visit him, and told me to join so I could get acquainted with them. As I walked through the door, I heard conversation and laughter coming from the room they were in. On the carved out wooden shelf by the door sat a potted welwitschia or tree tumbo, its two leaves draped on the floor like a long beard. It was clear the plant had been a gift from his former pupils. The Professor introduced them to me one by one, and then introduced me to them. They all looked different, yet somewhat alike, and just like the Professor they all had a habit of licking their lips as they spoke. Professor Su pretty much only did it to get rid of the spittle in the corners of his mouth. When he was making an emotion-laden point, spittle gathered in the corners of his mouth the same way foam did in that of a crab, after which he briskly stuck out his tongue to lick it off and prevent the saliva from spraying everywhere. His pupils, on the other hand, licked their lips for the sake of licking. They stuck out their tongues even in the absence of saliva. They had already inherited this habit of his.

All these former acolytes of Professor Su's had lived abroad, giving them an air of being exceptional. Within the room's confines, they altogether discussed worldly problems. The Dollar. The Euro. Oil. Stock prices. Nuclear Weapons. The situation in the Middle East. The latest information released by the Pentagon. And so on and so forth. Sometimes they threw in a few English, Spanish or French phrases. After tackling the major global issues, we started to debate the studies of ancient Chinese civilization and ranking senior academics according to their merit. As they decided on the order, they remembered to include Professor Su in their ranking of Masters of Chinese studies.

Professor Su chuckled, stating that he did not yet deserve to be ranked among immortals. The only one truly deserving of the epitaph of 'Grand Master', he said, was his teacher Zhu Xiantian. Acknowledging the latter's superiority, we naturally referred to him as *shigong*, the 'Master par excellence'. At age 90, he had come down with lung cancer. A scholar described by his peers as the 'soul of the academic world', he had been unable to put up with laying on his sickbed and existing only in a pathological sense, so he had hoped to die early and turn into a passing whiff of consciousness. When

Professor Su talked about him, his expression turned somber. He said Professor Zhu had been his mentor in college, and had always lived a life of scanty means.

'He only needed a place to eat and a place to stay to be able to immerse himself in his studies. Upon enrolling in college, I found out he was living in an old courtyard behind the school, and until then hadn't moved once. The school provided him with a small building to live in which he didn't want, saying that people are like trees once they get old: if you move them they wither.'

Professor Zhu had another quirky habit, he said: 'While I was working as his assistant, he put important things, or things he deemed important, in a little attic, which he never allowed others a single peek into. Despite suffering from a bad leg, he would drag his crippled limb into that room, where it took him ages to find what he was looking for. To this day, I still don't know what treasures he kept hidden in there.'

Professor Su looked into the distance, pondered for some time and said 'Professor Zhu felt greatly upset with the bankruptcy of Chinese traditional culture. To this day, I still recall how he wept bitter tears while holding on to remnant steles in the courtyard of his family's ancestral hall.'

Greatly moved by the tone of voice with which Professor Su looked back on his mentor, we all proposed to pay the bedridden Professor Zhu a visit. As we drove to the hospital, someone called saying that Mr Zhu had passed away at 2:28 p.m. Professor Su asked his students in the car to take him home. We were taken aback, unable to make out why Professor Su would want to turn back midway. Back at the house, he went inside and closed the door behind him, leaving us no choice but to smoke and chat under the tree shade as we sat outside, waiting. A while later, Professor came out wearing a black Sun Yat Sen-style jacket. He said 'Only with my tunic suit on can I comply with the ceremonial rites befitting of a disciple.'

*

On our way to the morgue, Professor Su gave directions from the front seat. I felt surprised at how well he knew the way to the morgue, even pointing out shortcuts and potential traffic jams. He told us that after having attended his fair share of funerals, he'd committed the directions to memory. When we arrived with the Professor, a group of expectant reporters clustered around him. He licked the spittle out of the corners of his mouth, and said into the microphone, 'It pains me to say that with the passing of Professor Zhu, a great deal of knowledge has been taken away from us. That ancient realm he'd once unlocked has now been sealed shut yet again. Distant and estranged, it's unclear how long it will take before someone reopens it, or whether it will forever remain out of reach.'

Professor Su then lauded Professor Zhu as one of the very few 'Indisputable Masters', and vowed to write a lengthy essay in which he would explain the extent of his trusted mentor's academic thought. After the interview, the reporters flocked elsewhere, evidently to surround Professor Su's fellow apprentice Wang Zhiyong, an archaeological expert who under Professor Zhu's tutelage had studied the ancient Para-Mongolic Khitan scripts. Professor Su did not take kindly to this man, and considered him a practitioner of an extinct branch of science, a pseudo-academic if you will. What he took particular issue with was that this man had once plagiarised an article which their teacher hadn't yet published. Professor Su pulled us aside and whispered, 'Seasoned sweet potato farmers dig close to the surface. Gravediggers dig even deeper than that. Those who dig the deepest are archaeologists. Wang Zhiyong, however, has no notable achievements to his name other than having turned the soil.'

Out of their utmost respect for Professor Su, his pupils unanimously looked down on all those he held in contempt. They looked at Wang Zhiyong in exactly the same way their teacher did.

Professor Wang Zhiyong had also spotted Professor Su, and came over to greet him out of courtesy. Speaking about recent developments, Wang Zhiyong let out a mysterious smile, saying that lately his interest of research had changed, and he had begun researching medical issues such as sneezing, belching and passing gas. At times, a 70-year-old is by no means more mature than a 17-year-old, and in this instance, the two of them seemed to have returned to boyhood from old age. Had they not been interrupted by a few other senior Professors, they might have ended up in a nasty war of words. While Professor Su was discussing with us the shift in academic thought that took place around the time of the May Fourth movement, Wang Zhiyong in turn discussed his research findings on flatulence with grave countenance. Professor Su covered his nose and turned away with an annoyed expression on his face. Because this was a gathering of distinguished figures, Professor Zhu's relatives had prepared the necessary calligraphy paraphernalia and asked Professors Su and Wang to each write a short eulogy. Professor Wang wrote a horizontal verse in the Khitan script, and Professor Su wrote his in Sanskrit. Even others wrote in Tokharian, Phags-pa, Dongba and Arabic. The presence of these long-lost scripts made it feel as if Professor Zhu had suddenly arisen from the dead. I felt a little ashamed for not being able to make out the meaning of a single character, but I could infer that they were all meant to express grief.

At nine in the morning, after I had just set foot in the Bamboo and Plum Blossom Pavilion, Professor Su flung a newspaper at me, flush with indignation. He said it featured a small obituary for Professor Zhu. I didn't get why the Professor was so upset, so I curiously scoured the paper for clues. The lengthier articles all covered the Euro Cup, whereas Professor Zhu's tiny obituary was barely noticeable in the bottom left corner. The header read, impressively, Renowned Linguist Zhu Xiantian Died of Illness Yesterday. In the sub-header, it said 'On his deathbed, he entrusted to his relatives the task of donating the RMB 20 000 advance for his new book to a charity organisation.' In the article's main body, another paragraph claimed that the director of a publishing house had solemnly promised to execute Professor Zhu's will.

Professor Su said that earlier that morning, Mr Zhu's eldest son Zhu Wengu had called him up, asserting that the old man hadn't left any will of the sort. Prior to his passing, Mr Zhu had merely shaken his fist and indignantly said a few words, mixed with a couple of expletives, but no one could make out who he was cursing at. He later fell into a coma, his blood pressure having reached 240 mmHg. Professor Su immediately confronted the reporter, but the latter, flustered as he was, passed the buck to the publishing house. The director of the publishing house said Professor Zhu's advance amounted to RMB 10 000 instead of the reported RMB 20 000, and that if his relatives didn't object, they would act in accordance with the 'testament' and donate the money to charity. As for who had put out that supposed testament, everything would become crystal clear if he just addressed his inquiry to Professor Zhu's second son. The matter smelled fishy, but Professor Su didn't mean to probe into it further, nor did he wish to meddle. Nevertheless, the case was obviously far from closed.

Not long after, Zhu Wengu called the Professor up again and said that despite not having been approved by Professor Zhu himself or his relatives (meaning his eldest son), they didn't want to fuss about the donation with the publisher any longer, seeing how it was for charity after all. A while later, the publisher called again, saying that the eldest son didn't need the advance anymore, yet it had somehow come to his attention that his father Mr Zhu was still owed RMB 10 000 in outstanding book royalties. The director explained that only a limited number of copies would be printed, considering only a handful of people were likely to understand Professor Zhu's book upon publication. He went on to say the royalties were determined based on the book price, distribution volume, royalty rates etc. In a word, it was decided by the invisible hand of the market. Mr Zhu's book couldn't be released on the mainstream market, and would only be acquired or collected by a tiny number of libraries and research institutes, which was why his relatives would barely take home any royalties. Professor Su lowered his voice and began to negotiate a deal with the director, and after repeated tradeoffs, they reached a verbal agreement. He put down the phone, and in the same breath shook his head and sighed. He made a call to Zhu Wengu, and said he had taken up the matter with the publisher, and that a one-off payment of RMB 10 000 would be transferred to their account.

Once the matter was settled, Professor Su walked over to tell me that Mr Zhu had helped him out back in the day when he was short of money. Needless to say, now that the Zhu family were struggling to make ends meet, he would do what he could to help them. The only thing he could do was to have his upcoming book released by that publisher, and to have his own RMB 10 000 advance remitted to Mr Zhu's relatives. What he regretted the most was that several uncompiled and unpublished manuscripts of Mr Zhu's were now unlikely to see the light of day. Professor Su tilted his chin backwards, uttered a long sigh, and said that with Professor Zhu gone, he felt like an ancient relic kept in a state of limbo.

'Years ago, I ventured into ancient times alongside Professor Zhu, and now I can't return. Woe to me,

I can't return, I can't return. . . ' Having said this several times in a row, he suddenly asked me whether I'd seen his wife come home.

I said I hadn't seen her, and a grave look formed on his face, leaving me at a loss for words. He walked through the living room into the study with his head hung low, stood still in front of one of the welwitschias and stubbed out his cigarette onto one of its leaves. He held the stub in place as if pressing someone's head, until it burned a little charred hole in the leaf. This was the first time I saw a cautionary trace of latent violence bubbling up within Professor Su.

On this sultry day, Professor Su hadn't opened the window, as if for fear that the slightest south wind would upset some sort of inner order. One door away, I could hear Professor Su's footsteps as he paced back and forth, but by the afternoon a slight fatigue made him drowsy. Xiao Wu, who had just finished washing glasses, came over and whispered to me, 'Just now, Professor Su started work on an article in memory of Professor Zhu, but after writing only the first two characters, he tossed his pen and stood up.'

'It's got to be the weather.' she said, 'It's a chore to mop the floor in this kind of hot and humid weather, let alone write essays.'

Xiao Wu had something in common with those grouchy, scorned housewives found in Tang-dynasty poetry, occasionally grumbling about the scorching heat. She was sure I felt equally uneasy, so she sat down next to me, and tirelessly shared her emotional tribulations with me. She mostly spoke about a poor and lazy toy-boy of hers, who she thought was a bore, and who had used the money she lent him to go whoring, only to get himself arrested. He had had the gall to beg her to fork out his bail money. She seized the opportunity to have me compliment her on her tolerance and benevolence. She had lost faith in life and men, and found life to be very tedious. She only confessed these things to me to blow off some steam. Eventually, though, chatting for the sake of it became a chore in itself. Such was also the case with me reading and writing out of boredom.

*

At Mr Zhu Tianxian's memorial service, Professor Su delivered a speech in his capacity as eldest pupil and head of the funeral rites committee. In his speech, he lamented nothing more than the fickleness of the weather and human affairs.

When the time came for Professor Wang to speak, he suddenly staggered and fell hard on the floor before he even got to the microphone, after which his arms and legs started convulsing and he passed out. The place was in chaos, prompting some attendees to call an ambulance, which rushed him to the hospital.

After the memorial service was abruptly called off, I accompanied Professor Su home. Given the stuffy weather, I proposed to have the research centre send a car, an offer which the Professor waved away saying there was no need to bother them, since we only needed to get on the Number 3 bus and then switch to the Number 9 to get home from the morgue. I ended up holding him by the hand as we got on the bus. One youngster tried to offer up his seat, but seeing the plaque that read 'courtesy seat for the elderly, pregnant or disabled', the Professor refused to sit in it. The kid muttered something to himself before sitting back down. I supported Professor Su with one hand, and held onto a support rail with the other, so I had no arms left to buy tickets. With no little effort, I fished out the change and handed it over to the angry and jittery sounding ticket seller.

After arriving at our stop, Professor Su gazed at the bus as it sped off, then suddenly sighed and said: 'There are two types of people who are in the habit of holding out their hands for change: the first are beggars, the second are bus ticket sellers. Beggars go about their days aimlessly. And what about ticket sellers? One might say they are never without direction, but if you piled up their everyday routines, you'd see they are equally aimless. How are we any different? Every day we seem to have stuff on our hands, but looking back we feel like we've accomplished nothing, idling away our whole lives.'

I didn't know what led Professor Su to this soliloquy. His tone was similar to when he'd read his morning eulogy, as if he was mourning the years gone by.

*

At nine the following morning, I arrived at the Bamboo and Plum Blossom Pavilion on time as per usual. With unkempt hair and a pair of slippers on, the Professor sat slumped on the couch, his head buried in a newspaper. He silently nodded at the sight of me. I didn't dare look him in the eye, and tiptoed into the small study. I took a seat after first wiping the table clean. Xiao Wu poured me a cup of tea, placed it on the table, then quietly told me that after waking up this morning, Professor Su had been in the strangest of moods. He hadn't gone out for his walk, and had declined to have breakfast. Instead, he just sat there staring blankly at his paper.

Through the glass window of the study, I could just make out the Professor's silhouette, as he frantically leafed through his newspaper. His morning lethargy and listlessness sank deeply into the couch's comfy creases.

He looked as though he'd had a lousy night's sleep. This was a rare sight, as Professor Su normally kept a regular sleep pattern, lived moderately, and didn't permit even the slightest exuberance. I suspected he suffered from what the papers called 'late-life depression'.

Before long, Professor Su sprang up from the couch, held the paper in front of me and told me he'd found three wrongly written characters. He had analysed the etymological origins and usage of all three characters, and concluded that that reading the papers lowered people's intelligence. That said, he kept looking at the paper. Those erroneous characters seemed to have become a grain of salt at the bottom of a shoe, or a piece of food annoyingly stuck between one's teeth. Finally, feeling fed up, he made a call to the editor-in-chief, who put him through to one of their copyeditors so he could relay his morning's worth of found errors.

At four in the afternoon, Professor Su didn't head into the kitchen timely to brew his customary pot of coffee. He just sat there the whole time, slumped on the couch, his expression weary. In that moment, I thought of something Professor Su himself had once said, 'If an elderly person's ability falls short of his wishes, he must outwit others. If, however, he's lacking in wit, he might as well be put up in the Alzheimer's ward.'

Looking at him now, he might as well have been an Alzheimer's patient. I got up and went to the kitchen, wanting to make him a cup of coffee. Once through the door, I saw the cutting board had a knife stuck in it at an angle. The 4 p.m. sunlight shone onto it and gave it a taunting quality. The knife reminded me of Mrs Su, who I hadn't seen in quite a while. I didn't know quite where she'd gone, nor did I dare ask. The sight of the knife brought to mind a murder case I'd read about in the paper the day before. A man had used a dog collar to strangle his wife to death, cut her up into eight big chunks with an electric saw, put her into a bag, then stored the bag in his basement freezer. The thought alone made my hand quiver. I reached for the fridge handle, but instead of opening it I merely grabbed it slightly as one would in preparation of a handshake, then walked out the room.

I took a cup of coffee and placed it in front of Professor Su, then made my way to the room in which Xiao Wu was chewing gum and listening to something in her headphones. She had one leg slung over the other, her knee bobbing rhythmically. She took the headphones off when she saw me, began to chat with me casually and asked whether I'd noticed Professor Su's irritation with a certain someone. Naturally, I knew she was hinting at Mrs Su. The day I'd first set foot in their home, I could see Mr Su and his wife were already on faux-friendly terms.

Xiao Wu confided in me rather cryptically that the lady of the house had gone back to her ex-husband.

I asked her who her ex-husband was, causing her to chuckle briefly and reply that it was Professor Wang Zhiyong. I'd never heard this mentioned by any of the colleagues in our centre, perhaps out of tactfulness to a man of erudition. What puzzled me was that if Wang Zhiyong had just had a cerebral hemorrhage, and was given emergency treatment on several occasions, wasn't Mrs Su asking for trouble by bestowing her palliative care on an old man who already had one foot in the grave? Xiao Wu seemed to read my mind, and said that just like Professor Su, Professor Wang Zhiyong had no next of kin. If he came to pass, she would be the rightful heir to his estate. Even more so, Mr Wang had once said to her that if she felt so inclined, he would leave all his family property to her. Xiao Wu compared the estates of both men, only to conclude that except for books and some old clocks, Professor Su didn't possess anything of value. Conversely, Wang Zhiyong's Ming-dynasty chair alone was worth several million. Xiao Wu threw a glance at Professor Su sitting absently in his parlour, and then imitated Mrs Su reclining in her chair, groaning some corny Tang-dynasty poem.

At dusk, Professor Su was still seated in the parlour. The TV, its volume turned way up, was showing a report on some disaster. The Professor's brows drew together in a frown and the wrinkles on his face were like rifts and cracks brought about by violent tremors. I could faintly see that on the surface he was following the catastrophic incident, but this was actually a distraction, a way to cover up the pain inside. When the TV cut to another program, Professor Su dragged his weary body into his study.

Xiao Wu then came out of the kitchen carrying a whole plate of hyacinth beans. The thin, long sleep marks on her face resembled silk sashes. Sitting down on the couch, she began stringing the beans at a snail's pace. She had her hands curled up in a way that resembled 'orchid fingers', a gesture achieved by Peking Opera performers by having the thumb touch the distal part of the middle finger and flexing the remaining fingers. The way I saw it, she only strung beans as a way to kill time. Her ten fingers with polished nails seemed sluggish and weak, as if they could only endure the weight of a single silk thread. Thus, for her, stringing beans was the same as threading a needle or repairing split ends of brittle hair. One might even compare it to me biting the bullet and perusing dull, ancient texts.

Through the glass, I could see an alternative, true-to-life projection of myself. Like me, she was also examining something, sometimes raising her head to glance over at the study. Her gaze seemed to conceal an expectation of some long-awaited truth that had never come to fruition. After she finished stringing the beans, she leaned forward toward a vase of wild pansies on the tea table and carefully picked off the withered petals, which she placed on top of the bean string pile. Perhaps tired of the housework, she recited yet another dreary sounding poem, as if memorising a few poems had taught her how to bemoan life.

As I was gearing up to head home, Xiao Wu stopped me, leaned over and whispered into my ear that Professor Su was feeling very depressed these days, and she would play a prank on him to cheer him up. Her mind made up, she went into Mrs Su's bedroom, put on the lady of the house's pajamas, huddled up onto the couch and assumed a pose of Mrs Su smoking. Then asked me, 'Do I look the part?'

I merely smiled and nodded, but deep down I felt she would never be able to approach Mrs Su's poise; hers was a mellow and unperturbed beauty, only exuded by a woman with enough seasons under her belt. Not long after, Professor Su came out of his study and saw a woman in pajamas curled up on the couch. Assuming it was his wife, he let out a quiet grunt. A little while later, he walked up to the couch with a bottle of ink, then opened it up, only to empty it on her head. Xiao Wu squealed, bounced up and scurried off into the bathroom. At that moment, I suddenly became aware of the subtle connection between this callous act and him previously putting out his cigarette stub on that plant leaf.

A few days later, something seemed to have gotten

into Professor Su. He broke with his conventional life patterns and taboos, and started behaving very unusually: he took naps during the day (occasionally dozing off on the couch, still holding the TV remote). After waking up, he neglected to brush his teeth, wash his face or even shave. His clothes and hair were a mess, he didn't bother to pick up the phone, nor did he do any reading or writing. The most drastic change was his sudden fondness for meat, be it mutton, pork, beef or chicken. He ate them all, and held his cutlery in an affectedly snobbish fashion. After gobbling down his meal, he became sleepy again, gravy still clotted in the corners of his mouth. The most puzzling of all was that he had tampered with the clocks in his study: he had set the Paris clock to Tokyo time, the New York one now ran synchronous to Beijing time, London time ran a little slower, whereas the Buenos Aires clock had been set forward and the Madrid dial permanently pointed to the twelve o'clock position. It was as if time all across the globe had gone mad along with him.

*

Our Centre Director originally wanted me to compile my conversations with Professor Su Jing'an in his later years, a task I hadn't quite gotten around to yet. Most of the time, I served as his secretary. For several days in a row, the Professor stayed indoors, not contacting anyone on the outside, so it was up to me to answer the slew of tedious incoming calls. One publisher called asking whether Professor Su wished to be included in the Encyclopedia of World Celebrities, meanwhile requesting us to transfer RMB 300 for said book as quickly as possible. One association of qigong masters wanted to bring Professor Su in as a consultant. Some college wanted him to attend their symposium. Some callers needed a signature, others called to make arrangements for literary contributions by the Professor, while even others just wanted to pick a quarrel. Currently, a reporter was on the line to ask him for personal comments on the spiritual heritage left behind by Professor Zhu Xiantian for future generations. As I was about to reject the invitation on the Professor's behalf, something both unexpected yet not entirely surprising happened.

From the study came the sound of Xiao Wu screaming. She came running out with her arms covering her bare chest. Just as teardrops formed in her eyes, the corners of her mouth revealed something of a triumphant, dare I say smug little smile. Not bothering to go over to her and ask what had transpired, I went straight into Professor Su's quarters. Scattered on the floor lay fragments of torn up blue book sleeves, alongside piles of books. Professor Su sat perched on a book pile with his head drooped down, absent-looking. It was as if his soul had left him. I bent over to help pick the books up off the floor, but the Professor raised his hand and waved feebly. Something seemed to be irremediably escaping from that overarching framework I knew to exist deep inside of him. He asked me if I knew why Xiao Wu had screamed just now. I had a hunch, but feigned cluelessness. He told me placidly that he had 'fondled' Xiao Wu. But the reason for him doing so, he said, was to treat the wound caused by cupid's arrow, and by no means had he meant for it to be perverse. 'Just like me,' he said, 'she's a pitiful human being who's gotten hurt.'

The following day, Professor Su told me he'd lost his house keys, and I needn't come in for work any longer. The following day and the day after that, I tried calling him, but to no avail. I later heard people say he had gone missing. Some said he'd gone back home to plant plum trees. Others claimed he had run off with the housekeeper. Some even likened him to Tolstoy, who had famously left his estate at a ripe age to live a peasant's life. They said his misery in old age was no less agonizing than that of Tolstoy, albeit minus the cold weather.

With Professor Su out of the picture, my work came to an abrupt halt. I had been influenced by the Professor and developed some strict life routines along the way. This sudden interruption made me lose my bearings, as if someone took away the latter half of a book I was indulged in, leaving me with a massive mental cliffhanger. Aside from being annoying, this of course gave me an unmanageable sense of anticipation. I called our Centre Director to report the issue. He hesitated, but decided it was best I stayed home and took a few days off, to wait and see how things went. After dinner, with nothing on my hands, I put my one-year-old in the pram and took him out for a casual stroll along the river. On our walk, I pointed out the willow trees and the sunset to him, the river and the flying birds. My son was babbling in an attempt to mimic my words. Halfway through our stroll, I saw an old person in a wheelchair being pushed in our direction. I looked closely and saw that it was Professor Wang Zhiyong.

His expression looked lifeless, and he was drooling out of the slanted corner of his mouth. Standing behind him was the long-lost Mrs Su, or should I say, Mrs Wang. She looked spritely as always with her hair gathered in a bun and her radiant complexion. She wore a cheongsam with a red plum blossom pattern. Behind them, the willow trees were swaying in the wind, which offset her figure all the more. I greeted her with 'Madam Professor', which she seemed to think was awkward and caused her mouth to pucker in a smile.

It was 'Madam Professor' who told me that after Professor Wang had fainted at the morgue several days earlier, he was left hemiplegic in spite of receiving timely treatment. The man sitting in front of me was no longer the old Mr Wang. Something seemed to have chipped away at his already slender face. His eyes and cheeks looked sunken, and his emaciated face with its protruding cheekbones emitted a morbid glow. His wisdom now seeped out from between his hair and wrinkles, and all that was left was a solidified obtuseness. I said to my son in the stroller, 'Say hi to grandpa Wang, will you?'

The boy and Professor Wang sat facing one another, with a century separating them. He sized up the old man with a peculiar look, opened his mouth, then let out some indiscernible gibberish. Wang Zhiyong suddenly looked jarred and started patting the wheelchair's armrests, urging 'Madam Professor' behind him, 'Go back. . . Let's go back home.'

*

Half a month after Professor Su's disappearance, I went back to work as suggested by our Centre Director. I resumed my normal routine; I worked and rested when I was supposed to, and of course I couldn't do without the obligatory Su-style afternoon tea. Apart from continuing to write out my conversations with Professor Su in his later years, I also took the time to sort out some of his typescripts that had never seen the light of day. While browsing through these writings, I came upon the recently completed first chapter of the Biography of Zhu Xiantian, entitled Listening to the Rain from Inside a Den of Ill Repute. This chapter dealt with some little-known anecdotes of the adolescent Zhu Xiantian.

It had never occurred to me that Mr Zhu had been a suave and rakish-looking charmer in his days. He was into the ladies, and would write countless flattering poems for the likes of actresses and prostitutes. He was fond of clothes, and wore a black silken shirt that rustled when he moved (Professor Su underscored that it was the kind worn by the cruel warlord character Nan Batian in the film Red Detachment of Women). These previously unknown teen antics brought to my attention Professor Zhu's toing-and-froing between the literate lassies and working girls of his day. Interestingly, some envy shone through in Professor Su's account of this particular phase in Mr Zhu's life.

Coincidentally, as I was reading Zhu Xiantian's biographical notes with great relish, his son and reputable veterinarian Zhu Wengu gave me a call to indicate he wanted to track down Professor Su. He spoke with great reservation, indicating that he didn't want me to spread the word. He went on to ask me about the Professor's whereabouts, a potential return date or even an address or telephone number of his. I told him I could give him none of these, and for the time being I also relied on others to try and get in touch with him. Zhu Wengu sighed deeply, saying he'd been going through troubled times lately, and the weirdest things had started happening. I asked him what exactly he was referring to. He hesitated for an instant then said, 'The other night, a police officer from my hometown called me up at home, saying my father had risen from the dead and appeared in front of our old house.'

I assured him, 'The dead aren't in the habit of dressing up as the living to prank other ghosts. Rather, people dress up as ghosts to fool other people, and they're a bunch of attention seekers.'

He said he didn't believe the police officer either, but what transpired later had left the police officer dumbstruck. On the day of the incident, the police officer's cyber investigation had revealed that the appearance of the elderly man trying to pass himself off as Zhu Xiantian didn't match the latter's description, despite his insistence on being one and the same person. I reassured him that the man had to be either a nutcase, or a con artist. He replied that if he was indeed a con-artist, there weren't any benefits to be gained, and if he was a crazy person, he must be the most level-headed lunatic he had ever come across.

According to Zhu Wengu's description, this erudite-looking person endowed with a prodigious memory was able to recite the main ideas of Mr Zhu's publications and books word for word. The officer had got in touch with Mr Zhu's relatives for identification purposes.

Zhu Wengu asked the old man a question only the real Professor Zhu could know, i.e. how big an advance Zhu Xiantian had received for the publication of his latest book. Remarkably enough, the old man came up with the correct amount, even explaining the ins-and-outs of his calculations.

For all his prior skepticism, Zhu Wengu now began to have his doubts. 'Could a person really come to life again in someone else's body?', he asked me.

I said that some things needed to be seen with one's own eyes, and that it would be best if he went over there to get closure in person. Still, Zhu Wengu began to prevaricate again. I told him that since Professor Su wasn't around, he didn't need to beat around the bush with me. He came out with it, 'I've heard a taped conversation with the old man, and he spoke in a voice similar to that of, dare I say. . . Professor Su. When you said just now that Professor Su ran off several days ago, I began to suspect it might be him.'

Having said that, he immediately rebuked, 'No, forget it, it can't be. I'm just making assumptions at this point.'

I asked him to have the police officer get in touch with me so we could talk about this old man who bore such likeness to Professor Zhu Xiantian. After hearing the police officer describe the man's facial features, I filled in the remaining sketch, to which he repeatedly replied 'That's right, that's right.'

I then had him play the taped conversations with the old man back to me. There was no doubt about it, this was Professor Su's voice. Although he sounded hoarse, I could tell it was him. During the conversation, he would call himself 'Zhu Xiantian', something I couldn't comprehend in the slightest. The officer said the old man looked normal, so they couldn't take him into custody, nor could they bring him to a psychiatric clinic. All they could do was put him up temporarily at a nursing home. I now felt the need to pay a visit to the hometown of Zhu Xiantian.

That same evening, Zhu Wengu and I headed to South Zhejiang on the same train, where we slept in the same carriage. Aside from his howl-like snoring, it was the animal fur odor emitted by this seasoned veterinarian that kept me up all night. By the time we got to the station, I was still in a state of sleepless trance. Before we even got to our hotel, we met up with a local police officer surnamed Song. Officer Song told us that 'the old man' had suddenly started to suffer convulsions the night before, so they'd brought him to the Municipal

People's Hospital. We rushed to the hospital in a cab without a single halt.

It was in room 301, bed number 4, that I saw Professor Su, his face all haggard-looking and his hair a mess. I walked up to his bed, grabbed his hand, and kept silent. The skin on his hand felt hardened, and his trim and yellowing fingernails had dirt underneath them. At that point, the joy of reuniting with a long-lost friend must have spilled from my eyes, whereas his expression seemed like he had just laid eyes on a stranger. Instead of being moved to tears as I had expected him to be, he looked tremendously tranquil. Seeing him peer at me over the frame of his glasses brought to mind a line in Su Shi's poem Former Ode to the Red Cliff we used to learn in school, which went '[. . .] over ten thousand acres of dissolving surface which streamed to the horizon [. . .]'.

His memory appeared to have been affected by some mysterious force. I didn't know what to say at first, nor did he, his expression still vacant. Our God-given muscles are more developed than those of any other creature, meaning that humans have a dynamic range of expressions, but Professor Su's face revealed nothing. Seeing Zhu Wengu standing behind me, his eyes lit up for a second, but he then said in a relatively flat tone, 'How. . . how come you're here too?'

Who did this 'you' refer to? Zhu Wengu leaned in and

asked 'Do you know who I am?', to which Professor Su replied in a nasal voice, 'Nonsense, how would I not recognize my own flesh and blood?'

There was nothing exaggerated about the way he said this, making Zhu Wengu seem like the more confused out of the pair. Zhu Wengu let out a sniggering laugh, which he managed to suppress instantly. When Professor Su talked, he came across as lucid, of sound mind and well-spoken, and it was hard to make out anything wrong with him. Every word I said, on the other hand, now felt like a lie, making me somewhat skeptical of this whole operation we had undertaken. In the end, Professor Su said, 'You guys go ahead and leave. I'm not ill, I don't need you to keep me company.'

My insomnia-induced fatigue had not yet passed, and as I exited the room, it felt like I was awaking from a dream. At the suggestion of officer Song, Zhu Wengu and I went to see the hospital's brain surgeon, who said that no definitive conclusion could be drawn yet in regards to Professor's medical condition. What was certain, though, was that his brain had at some point suffered blunt trauma, and some blood clots hadn't entirely cleared up. This was corroborated by the findings in officer Song's investigation: Professor Su's head had gotten injured when some tattooed drunk kids had hurled rocks at him. But I couldn't say for sure that the Professor's unusual behavior could be traced back to a few dumb rocks. The doctor was also merely inferring that this incident may have brought on the patient's neurological disorder.

I asked the doctor what symptoms a patient with a neurological disorder would display. He didn't answer directly, but said with a stern look, 'I've never encountered any patient the likes of Mr Zhu, or should I say, Mr Su. Although he's mistaken about his own identity, he has absolutely no misgivings about his claims. He's an intelligent and bookish man. I've spoken to him, and I cannot help but be utterly impressed at his insightful views on medical science.'

Zhu Wengu interrupted him saying, 'If him treating me like his own son doesn't point to serious brain malfunction, then what does?'

The doctor turned around and asked 'Who's this?'

I told him it was Mr Zhu Wengu, son of Mr Zhu Xiantian, to which the doctor replied 'Well, that explains it. If he calls himself Zhu Xiantian, it's only right that he would address you as his son.'

Zhu Wengu chuckled, but it took him considerable effort.

The next day, I went over to Professor Su to bring him breakfast. He glanced at me and said, 'I'd like some congee and a salted duck egg.'

I nodded and immediately headed out to buy what he had asked for. I ran into Zhu Wengu in the spacious entrance hall of the hospital. He asked me if Professor Su was awake. He couldn't wait to have a serious tête-à-tête with him. I told him I'd join after I'd bought the congee and salted duck egg. He suddenly grabbed me by the sleeve and asked, 'How come even his taste has become identical to my father's? Before his death, dad always used to say he had no ambition of becoming a wealthy big shot in his lifetime, that eating congee already placed him above the celestial beings up high, and that adding two salted duck eggs would leave him utterly contented. The only thing that changed was the duck eggs got increasingly saltier.'

I told him, 'How about you go in and chat with him first, and I'll join after.'

As I walked into the room carrying the congee and salted duck eggs, I saw Zhu Wengu wipe tears out the corners of his eyes, ostensibly overcome with melancholy. As I opened up the boxed meal, Zhu Wengu took a table spoon and said he wanted to personally feed Professor Su the congee. That way he still came off as a filial son feeding his old man his medicinal blend. After he was done feeding him the congee, we left the room. He told me Professor Su's expression was as pure as the Buddha's, much like his own father's.

'The likeness is striking', he said.

*

Both the doctor and outside observers all had their
own take on Professor Su's mental state. Some said he
was possessed by a demon, others said it was voodoo, a
neurological disorder, a memory transfer, a feigned mental disorder, escapism or madness brought on by qigong
breathing practice, while some even claimed his brain
had been tampered with by extraterrestrials. I couldn't
say for sure which version was closer to the truth. The
fact was that his brain had been occupied by something
unknowable that lay beyond my comprehension, and
which he himself couldn't make heads or tails of either.

After his afternoon nap, I took Professor Su out for
a walk. It was just the two of us, strolling in the quiet
courtyard downstairs of the inpatient ward. I scrutinized
Professor Su's every move. I thought that if he had
genuinely retained his sanity, he'd stop pretending on his
own accord during our time alone, and he'd tell me what
intentions were behind his behavior. However, Professor
Su remained silent, as if liberated from the necessity of
moving his tongue. I myself became one with the swaying trees beside him. As light shone through the trees,
it skimmed across my eyes, and the distant view of the
forest seemed like a mirage.

While Professor Su was undergoing treatment at
the hospital, I accompanied Zhu Wengu on a visit to

Zhu Xiantian's old home. Few people could be seen in the countryside, and the thick shades of densely foliated trees lay spread out over the land, while a slight afternoon breeze blew imperceptibly. In an overgrown spot, we found the old site where the Zhu family had once lived. Out here, the Zhu's had originally been a wealthy and influential family. None of the old houses were around now, except for the dilapidated remains of an old porch. An elderly man who had seen us gesturing at the entrance, tottered over to us with his cane and asked us where we were from, and what the nature of our visit was. Without introducing himself, Zhu Wengu asked the man if he was acquainted with Zhu Xiantian, the senior head of the Zhu family. Upon hearing Zhu Xiantian's name, the old man stuck out his thumb and said he knew him to be a terrific man.

Pleased to hear this, Zhu Wengu went on to ask if he knew what his father was like as a young lad. The old man replied he was a smart and exotic looking young fellow who had captured the hearts of countless young ladies. At this point, the old man suddenly lowered his voice, and said Mr Zhu was incredibly generous. 'Back when I was still a vendor of salted duck eggs', he reminisced, 'your father was a frequent patron of mine, and he even took me to a brothel once.'

Zhu Wengu, who was now having a hard time listening to these stories, turned his head and used his hand to fan in front of his nose, as if he'd picked up on a bad smell coming from the old man's mouth. The old man wasn't done yet. He leaned on his cane and came up to him, saying that 'Afterwards, your old man lost money dealing in silk, and the family was forced to sell off the ancestral home and move to the countryside. In hindsight, it was a good thing he lost the family property, otherwise they would've paid for it with their lives later on down the line. At the time, Mr Zhu had two choices: either become a monk, or go abroad. After giving it much thought, he still chose to go abroad, and disappeared without a trace.'

Zhu Wengu asked if he had ever returned to the village since. The old man shook his head and said he hadn't seen him ever since, nor heard others speak of his return. 'But', he said, 'I did see a weird old fellow show up who tried to pass himself off as Mr Zhu. I presumed he was out to scam people out of their land and saw right through him, so I had my grandson report it to the police, who took him into the city precinct for questioning.'

Zhu Wengu and I thanked the old man, and walked along the ramshackle wall footing of the old Zhu residence. Zhu Wengu said it would be lovely if such a huge place could be turned into a livestock farm, and it was a pity to see it fall into disuse.

*

Despite its location on hometown soil, this plot of land wasn't the Zhu clan's any longer. Zhu Wengu had already purchased his return ticket and didn't intend to stay much longer. I treated him to a meal in a rustic little bistro. We ordered some of the local specialties, and we each got two bowls of yellow rice wine, which we sipped on as we chatted. Zhu Wengu was a sluggish guy: granted he had alcohol, he would sit there motionlessly like a stake in the ground. After his tongue came in contact with the flavorful liquid, he started to feel utterly at ease. Of course, most of our conversation revolved around his family's affairs.

He told me he hadn't known his father as well as the rest of us did, which made me feel guilty. This old veterinarian hit the nail on the head, since I didn't detect any of his father's bookishness and scholarly refinement in him. He bravely admitted to me that he was only similar to his father in appearance, but that Professor Su resembled him in spirit. Disregarding their physical differences, one might believe Professor Su to be his father.

I indicated to Zhu Wengu that I agreed with him. I said that out of all animals, apes bear the greatest physical resemblance to humans, but that mice actually share 99 per cent of their genetic makeup with humans.

As a vet he could give his professional take on this animal analogy.

He said that aside from a biological connection, he and his siblings didn't seem to have inherited any of their father's genes. Because of the era they'd grown up in, the Zhu brothers and sisters were never able to spend enough time with their father to receive his intellectual nourishment. In the ensuing years they had simply worked low-grade jobs like butcher, midwife, etc. Meanwhile, because of flimsy family ties, their characters grew more distant with each passing day, their differences ending up greater than those between humans and apes.

Zhu Wengu said his mother had always held his father in contempt, which absurdly enough led the rest of the family to reserve particular loathing for knowledge. After their father's book collection got seized, they made sure to wipe their behinds with every last sheet of paper that had writing on it.

While on the topic of the past, I detected obvious traces of remorse and empathy in his voice, and tried to put myself in his place. He even went on to scold his own younger brother, calling him 'lowlier than a dirty swine'. I could only imagine what feuds existed between the Zhu brothers.

I then proceeded to take up the most pressing matter at hand with Zhu Wengu, 'If we bring Professor Su back, who will take care of him in his daily life?'

I just brought up the issue, not intending to drag him into it.

Zhu Wengu smiled thinly and said, 'Surely you don't expect me to take him in and look after him as if he were my real father?'

Naturally, I didn't object to living with him in the Su residence, and inheriting his family possessions. If that were the case, it would be hard to say who was providing for whom. After all, ahem, I wasn't getting any younger myself. . .

I held up a bowl of yellow rice wine and said to Zhu Wengu, 'There's something you may not know. Professor Su helped negotiate that RMB 10 000 in royalties you originally demanded from Zhu Xiantian's publisher. Even though it fell through in the end, he still conceded and gave his own manuscript to the publisher. They took RMB 10 000 off his advance and transferred it to you guys. According to him, it was partly inspired by having studied in utter destitution, and partly intended as a means of paying back his mentor.'

After hearing me say this, I could swear steam was bellowing from his mouth. At first I thought Zhu Wengu would be moved to tears after he heard what I said, but little did I expect he would heave a deep sigh and say, 'We would've been better off without the money. Because of it, us siblings, we all had a falling out.'

I smiled wryly, without uttering a sound. After lunch, Zhu Wengu let out a booze-induced belch, put one hand on my shoulder and said to me earnestly, 'I'm taking the afternoon train back. For now, all I can do is leave the matter of Professor Su in your hands.'

When he left, he gave me a forced smile, along with an ambiguous hand gesture.

*

I got back to the hospital, tied up all the loose ends concerning Professor Su's hospital expenses, then went to an internet bar and sent word to the housekeeper Xiao Wu via QQ Messenger. I explained to her the circumstances that had befallen Professor Su, and what I was intending to do next, in the hopes that she could rejoin Professor Su as soon as possible. But Xiao Wu's response left me baffled.

She said she had just completed a seminar in Beijing on how to become a high-level caregiver. She'd even made an appearance on a caregivers' talent show on TV. Her asking price was now different than before, and the jaw-droppingly high amount she mentioned left me speechless. I went offline, and gathered that from here on out I would discontinue my dealings with Xiao Wu.

After dinner, I got a text message from Xiao Wu saying she could go back to taking care of Professor Su, but under one – frankly laughable – condition. She would return to Professor Su's side not as a kitchen maid, but to take the place of Mrs Su, effectively becoming the lady of the house. She said the reason she'd made this decision was because Professor Su still had some savings set aside. She hoped to get a reply from me before she had a change of mind. But I told her I wasn't at liberty to give my consent on the matter, and that even Professor Su himself was not in a position to agree to this.

Two days later, it was time for us to head back to the city. The slow hours of the night were the hardest to kill. Under the weak lamplight, Professor Su and I sat facing each other. I had no clue what oddness inhabited his mind. I was under the false impression that Professor Su was playing a game of hide-and-seek with himself, that he was searching for himself amid his own labyrinthine confusion, but that he had found his very own teacher Zhu Xiantian in the process, and decided to become him.

There are various ways to prove that A doesn't equate B, but in this instant I would much rather believe that he was indeed Mr Zhu. When he claimed to be Zhu Xiantian, he seemed way more loveable. Even though he was blatantly lying, I had to admit he was an odd yet fascinating fellow. The whole night long, he talked to me about scholarly figures, giving his opinion on such scholars as Qian Mu, Pang Pu, Li Zehou, Su Jing'an and Wang Zhiyong. He talked about Su Jing'an a lot and in great detail.

He asked me whether I knew why Su Jing'an's given name was Jing'an. I didn't know the answer, so he went, 'He's called Jing'an because he was frail and got sick a lot as a child, so his parents named him after a monk in a local village temple, which was said to ward off evil.'

On the topic of Mrs Su, he said 'Su Jing'an and Wang Zhiyong were my favourite pupils. She was the reason both men had a falling out. She'd been a student of Wang Zhiyong's first. Over time, they started having feelings for each other, so they decided to tie the knot. After a few years, she left him and became Su Jing'an's student, and they fell in love at the drop of a hat, which was a boon for both of them.'

He mainly spoke about the past, yet drew a blank on a whole entire period after that. He spoke in a low voice, murmuring along to the rustling of leaves outside the train window.

In the middle of his rant, he suddenly stopped, stared at me, gazing fixedly for a brief moment, then asked a question which took me aback, 'Who might you be?'

I dwelled on the question for some time, then suddenly the answer dawned on me.

I altered my sitting position, and calmly responded: 'It is I. Su Jing'an.'

A Story of Friendship and Trauma by Chi Zijian

Ji Lianna passionately tends to her flower garden and avoids looking back at her life with remorse. Xiao'e does not know the first thing about plants and cannot stop thinking about her past. Eighty-year-old Ji Lianna is a child of the Jewish diaspora, and young Xiao'e is not sure whether she is human at all. The two women could not be more different. Yet, in a numbingly cold Harbin flat in an old Russian villa, an unlikely friendship blossoms between them. Soon their dark histories come back to haunt them as they realise they have more in common than just a shared address.

Translated from the Chinese by Poppy Toland

Fleeing Xinhe Street

by

ZHE GUI

Translated from the
original Chinese by
Ana Padilla Fornieles

PENGUIN BOOKS

UK | USA | Canada | Ireland | Australia
India | New Zealand | South Africa | China

Penguin Books is part of the Penguin Random House group of companies
whose addresses can be found at global.penguinrandomhouse.com

Penguin
Random House
PENGUIN BOOKS

This paperback edition published by Penguin Group (Australia), 2019

1 3 5 7 9 10 8 6 4 2

Text copyright © Zhe Gui, 2019

Translated from the Chinese by Ana Padilla Fornieles

Produced with Writers Association of Zhejiang Province

Originally published in Chinese as *Pao Lu* with the Writers Association of
Zhejiang Province and in People's Literature

The moral right of the author has been asserted.

Cover design by Di Suo © Penguin Group (Australia)
Text design by Steffan Leyshon-Jones © Penguin Group (Australia)
Printed and bound in China by RR Donnelley Asia Printing Solutions Ltd.

ISBN: 9780734398680

penguin.com.au

MIX
Paper from
responsible sources
FSC   FSC™ C144853
www.fsc.org

About the Translator

Ana Padilla Fornicles (Spain, 1989) graduated in Translation and Interpreting Studies from the University of Granada. She is based in Beijing, where she combines her work in the cultural field with her literary and artistic career and her involvement in the local literary scene.

Wang Wuxian

Wang Wuxian enjoyed making fun of his physical defects and he happily let friends laugh at his expense, too. He was colour-blind, so in his world, neither green nor red existed. He once wore a pair of bright red trousers to a get-together. His friends were aware of his condition and intentionally tested him at every gathering.

'Wang Wuxian, look at the clothes I am wearing today. What colour are they?'

Wang Wuxian would stare intently for a moment. 'They're green, dammit!' he would confidently state.

As soon as he would open his mouth, he would be met with his friends' laughter, and would immediately laugh along as well.

Besides his colour-blindness, Wang Wuxian also had aesthetic standards that differed from those of other people. The average man deems a melon seed-shaped face, wasp waist and perky buttocks to be the three main criteria of a beautiful woman. To Wang Wuxian's eye, however, a beauty would be adorned with a face shaped like an apple, a waist wide like a bucket and round buttocks. Therefore, whenever they saw an unfortunate-looking woman, his friends would egg him on. 'Wang Wuxian, here's your type of girl.'

Wang Wuxian would swiftly glance at the woman only to hang his head in shame, and then laughter would ensue again.

Wang Wuxian's home served as a shelter for plenty of small, abandoned cats and dogs. He quite simply could not bear seeing tiny animals wandering the streets. Their sight would move him to tears and he just had to hug them all the way back home.

His friends said his place was a zoo, but he laughed and said it was more like a kennel. In any case, his friends' teasing was clearly well-meaning. After all, they knew that a man who showed love for all stray kittens and puppies was a man that would never hurt his friends.

In Zhejiang Province's Wenzhou City on Xinhe Street, Wang Wuxian was a nobody — unlike those that he had dealings with. They were entrepreneurs of all sizes who were frequently featured in newspapers and on TV. They would also often meet and eat with the bigwigs of Xinhe Street and go abroad together. In a certain way, one could say that those fat cats dominated the fate of Xinhe Street. Sometimes, Wang Wuxian would be under the illusion that he too could dictate the fate of Xinhe Street. He would only entertain such a misconception in his mind after drinking; without alcohol involved, he could understand his own position just right.

Wang Wuxian enjoyed his wine, but there was only so much alcohol he could tolerate. Once he had downed half a bottle, his cheeks would redden and resemble a tomato. At that point, no matter how much others encouraged him, he would hold on to the glass with his left hand and sway his right, laughing, 'No more, no more.'

Prodding or calling him a son of a bitch for refusing to drink was all in vain. He would laugh, putting down his glass and rolling his sleeves up to reveal his white, plump arms. Twisting his body, he would rebuke everyone, 'Look! Look! All red! Even my butt cheeks!'

The crowd would roar with laughter.

Wang Wuxian was mocked by his friends for another reason: he had yet to marry. Wang Wuxian was forty years old. A man his age with no wife – wasn't that a little strange? How did he deal with sex? Everybody just knew that he never went anywhere that could be considered a place of recreation, nor did he have a girlfriend. This made it even harder for people to understand him. Could it be that he was a homosexual? Nobody had ever seen him hitting on any male friend, and even if there was a little softness to his movements, a certain mildness to his tone and a little charm to his gaze, he had never gone a step further in his behaviour. At times some friend would tease him a little by asking him, 'Wang Wuxian, are you straight? Are you actually all right down there?'

With a loving look at his friend, Wang Wuxian would giggle, 'Damn, how about you come to see by yourself?' Then he would pause. 'You know what, forget it. Your wife would beat me to death,' he would add.

Everybody would burst out laughing again.

It is easy to make fun of yourself. The challenge lies in allowing others to laugh at you, too. This requires fixed boundaries. Wang Wuxian became an indispensable part of any given get-together with friends. If he didn't show up, everybody would gloomily ask, 'Why is Wang Wuxian not here?' Their voices would have a tinge of infinite loss, yet as soon as the atmosphere livened up, he was promptly forgotten.

Most of the time, Wang Wuxian was an easy-going person, someone who laughed everything off. However, as soon as anything related to his 'career' came up, that character of his became a stream of water. His words wouldn't stop flowing and he wouldn't stop his offensive until he had achieved whatever purpose he had set his mind to. At such times, the softness of his character transformed into an uninterrupted attack. He had built his career with this 'soft-hard' approach.

Wang Wuxian's so-called career was, in fact, a guarantee company named the One Plus One Guarantee Company.

'Why call it the One Plus One Guarantee Company? Does it have any profound meaning?' people asked him.

'No, not really,' he laughed. 'If there's any meaning to it, it'd be that first of all my surname is Wang, and if you add one to one, you get the character for my surname. Then there's also this beautiful goal of mine. I want all my customers to get high returns from their dealings, and for their wealth to keep increasing. I wish for their investments to keep rising steadily, like a brick wall.'

In fact, Wang Wuxian's beautiful goal was not a fantasy. His customers did indeed get great returns from their dealings with him, sometimes even huge ones. How was that possible? Business is risky for sure, and the higher the possibility of payback, the higher the risk. This is common knowledge.

If one wanted to delve into the reasons, they would have to start from the nature of the One Plus One Guarantee Company. Generally speaking, whenever an individual or a company seeks a loan from a bank, the bank requires that a third party vouches for them in order to reduce the institution's risk. This is where a guarantee company comes in. In compliance with the bank's requirements, a guarantee company issues the borrower the relevant credentials, carries out a review and submits the audited materials to the bank. Once the bank has reviewed the materials and granted the loan, the guarantee company proceeds to collect the corresponding service fees. In this process, guarantee companies usually charge a 2 per cent service fee. This fee does not have a high rate of return and it is even more unlikely to have a huge one. However, Wang Wuxian's One Plus One Guarantee Company was in the business of borrowing and lending money. To sum it up, his guarantee company did the exact same business as that of a bank. According to the laws of China, it is illegal for a guarantee company to borrow and lend money. Needless to say, Wang Wuxian wasn't oblivious to this fact. However, Wang Wuxian knew something else with even greater certainty – this risk involved huge profits. The loan interest of a bank stands at approximately 0.6 per cent, yet that of the guarantee company amounted to 6 per cent and could even rise to a maximum of 10 per cent. Even though some defaulted on these loans, this level of interest rate guaranteed high profit margins. Such a high rate of return was indeed worth the risk.

This posed just one problem; with such a high interest rate, who would possibly turn to Wang Wuxian's company to take out a loan? Moreover, where did the money that Wang Wuxian loaned out come from?

Enterprises were the target of Wang Wuxian's loan business. Xinhe Street was a place where privately owned businesses thrived. According to the statistics of the Department of Industry and Commerce, there were 100000 small or medium-sized enterprises and 350000 small-scale privately owned businesses. Most of them were engaged in selling leather shoes, clothing, eyeglasses, lighters, low-voltage electrical appliances, packaging and printing services, amongst others. An abundance of enterprises comes with competition. In order to be successful, both businesses and small privately owned enterprises need to develop and expand. Development and expansion need financial support. Oftentimes, entrepreneurs and business owners turn to a bank to ask for a one-year loan. Upon the one-year deadline, they must repay the loan prior to reapplying for a new one. However, having invested the borrowed money in production, recovering the costs in one year is out of the question. How could they possibly repay the bank? At moments like these, they might think of a guarantee company such as Wang Wuxian's, with his comparatively simpler procedures. Those who borrowed money from Wang Wuxian tended to be mostly friends' acquaintances and they would get the money straight away. Banks are nowhere near as fast. According to the usual procedures, and even after completing all formalities, it will take at least half a month's time to get the money. Wang Wuxian knew that those who turned to him needed the money urgently, so he raised the interest rate by ten times higher than that of the bank. Under normal circumstances, entrepreneurs repaid the loan within one month; the fastest of them even the day after. Traditional industries such as those of Xinhe Street typically saw a net profit of about 10 per cent. Entrepreneurs could not afford to bear such high-interest rates for a long time.

Enterprises were also the target of Wang Wuxian's borrowing business. Generally, it was all about a few big enterprises. Large enterprises have a relatively abundant capital flow and Wang Wuxian gave them an interest rate of 3 per cent. This was a huge amount in comparison to the 0.6 per cent offered by banks. A considerable number of businesses saw through the mysterious principles involved in this process. Therefore, after taking a loan from the bank, they would invest part of that money in their production and place the rest in Wang Wuxian's guarantee company. Every month, they raked in considerable interest from Wang Wuxian, which was much easier than doing actual business.

Individuals represented yet another source of Wang Wuxian's profits. They mostly came from governmental agencies, including some small business owners and self-employed individuals. These people mortgaged their houses or business facilities with the bank and took the money they obtained to Wang Wuxian's guarantee company. Depositing RMB one million, for instance, allowed them to get RMB 360 000 back in interest in one year, with only RMB 70 000 in annual interest left to pay back to the bank. These were debts that everyone was willing to take on and it was business everybody was willing to get into.

Despite it all, Wang Wuxian fled to the United States just when his guarantee company was at its peak of prosperity. His escape was prompted by issues within one of the links of the One Plus One Guarantee Company. Guarantee companies resemble chains, with each and every link tied together. If trouble arises with any of them, the entire chain falls apart. There were many reasons as to why there was trouble with the guarantee company, yet Wang Wuxian believed that the most direct one was that banks had tightened up on money. As a result, all initially promised loans had faded.

Trouble first came through one of Wang Wuxian's clients, the owner of a glasses factory. His business in Xinhe Street was within the upper-middle range, yet he hoped to reach the top and expand it to the dominant position of a big brand. His plans earned him the support of a local bank that granted him a RMB twenty million loan. With that capital he introduced a new assembly line, upon which the factory's output doubled in the first year, with the annual profit increasing from the original RMB 1.5 million to 3.5 million. Maintaining that momentum, the factory would have needed only six years to pay off the bank loan. According to the regulations of the bank, after the first-year loan expired, the glasses factory had to repay twenty million to the bank prior to initiating the procedures for a new loan. Regarding access to their new loan, the bank initially told the glasses factory that they would have an answer for them within five working days. Needless to say, the glasses factory did not have twenty million ready to repay the bank. All they could do was turn to Wang Wuxian through friends for a loan.

Wang Wuxian knew this customer would have a short-term turnover and the customer needed the money badly. Therefore, he stipulated a 5 per cent interest rate to begin with. Furthermore, he stated that no matter whether the other party repaid the money in thirty days or in three days, this interest would be calculated on a monthly basis. The glasses factory would owe him RMB one million in interest. The glasses factory owner had no choice but to turn to Wang Wuxian, and all he could do was accept his conditions. On that very same day, he got twenty million from Wang Wuxian. One week later, he repaid twenty-one million to Wang Wuxian. Once the second-year loan expired, the glasses factory owner went to Wang Wuxian again. This time around, Wang Wuxian increased his monthly interest rate to 6 per cent. The glasses factory owner signed the contract while clenching his teeth. The glasses factory repaid twenty million to the bank, only to be suddenly notified that due to orders from the top, all lending was temporarily suspended. The glasses factory owner felt weak at the knees as soon as he heard this. He sought out the head of the bank, who was willing to help but ultimately unable to do so. The glasses factory owner left the bank empty-handed and reconsidered his position over the next week. He did not manage to figure out how to repay those twenty million to Wang Wuxian. This, however, he knew for certain – if he dragged this on for too long, Wang Wuxian's interest rates would soon eat up his glasses factory. Eventually, he came up with a solution. He gave his workers two days off and arranged a trip for them to the Nanxi River scenic area on behalf of the trade union. Whoever refused to take part in the activity would be fined RMB 200 daily. In the lapse of those two days, he sold off all machinery, left a sum of money to cover the workers' wages and took his family to seek refuge with relatives in Australia.

Once the glasses factory owner fled, the leather shoe factory owner, the garment factory owner, the lighter factory owner, the low-voltage electronic appliances factory owner, the packaging and printing factory owner and all the rest of them fled too. Subsequently, an even bigger problem arose – upon learning about the escape epidemic, the customers who had originally placed their money in Wang Wuxian's hands also grew agitated. They all went to Wang Wuxian and demanded to withdraw their capital.

Wang Wuxian could not think of a solution to this crisis. If the money that went out did not come back, the money he had taken could not be repaid either. All he could do was take the money from the guarantee company and flee to the United States. Wang Wuxian did not want to do that. He could not stand the thought of those poor kittens and puppies being forced to wander the streets again if he left. In order to find a new place for them, Wang Wuxian knocked at countless neighbours' doors and did not stop until he managed to find new homes for each and every one of them.

Wang Wuxian left Xinhe Street for Shanghai in the dead of night. There, he boarded a flight bound for the United States. He knew this was his farewell to Xinhe Street.

Hu Weidong

Wang Wuxian's escape affected Hu Weidong the most. Hu Weidong was one of those people who Wang Wuxian believed could dictate the fate of Xinhe Street. He was also Xinhe Street's most famous leather shoe business owner.

Hu Weidong's Zhenxing Leather Shoe Company had been originally founded by his father, Hu Zhenxing. Hu Zhenxing had made himself quite the name in the leather shoe-making trade on Xinhe Street. Back then there was no specific word for the concept of a famous brand, but being able to wear a pair of leather shoes made by good old Zhenxing was considered very much a *thing*. At that time, when young people from Xinhe Street tied the knot, heading to Zhenxing's to order a pair of leather shoes was a must. At the age of fourteen, Hu Weidong started as an apprentice in his father's workshop. By the time he took over, he had already transformed the work-shop into a factory. When he started working alongside his father, they were the only ones in the workshop. By the time the company went to Hu Weidong, there were already over sixty workers at the factory, which was the main supplier for various shops and a wholesale point for various more. Later on, Hu Weidong managed to turn the factory into a company, bringing in an assembly line from Italy, growing the staff to over a thousand workers and ultimately opening more than two thousand franchised stores nationwide. Hu Weidong was also elected president of the Xinhe Street Leather Shoe Association and thus became an ambassador of the trade at Xinhe Street. He was a symbol. He was consistently invited to take part in government economy-related meetings. The banking department also took special care of him and took the initiative to grant him credit and loans.

From his early childhood, Hu Weidong had always been obedient. For as long as he could remember, he had known that he would have to devote his life to the leather shoe business. He only attended junior middle school for a year before his father made him drop out. He did not ask why, he simply focused on learning the art of leather shoemaking from his father. When he became an apprentice, he played second fiddle to his father for the first year. His father did not teach him any technical skills; instead, he made him use his eyes to learn. Hu Weidong simply shadowed his father. He would wake up and have his meals with his father. Where his father used a big glass to drink water, he would use a small one. He went to the loo when his father did, and shook his willy after peeing when his father did. Hu Zhenxing wore a black leather cap, a pair of black leather gloves and a black leather apron, which became Hu Weidong's outfit as well. Had it not been for Hu Weidong's smaller frame, the pair would have been difficult to tell apart.

Hu Weidong felt he was not a clever man. He always heeded his elders, but he also asked a lot of questions. If he saw his father measuring their clients' feet, he would question why he did it his way. If he saw his father cutting leather, he would ask why one side he cut was thicker than the other. If he saw his father glueing components of a shoe together, he would ask which way was the right way to do so. If he saw his father stitching shoes with a needle, he would ask what was the appropriate needlework and what would the right stitch length be for each shoe.

Initially, his father would not reply to any of his questions, calling him by his side to watch instead. Hu Weidong was not discouraged; he kept his eyes open and his mouth free from idleness. His father ignored his questions, beginning to answer them only a year later. There were about sixty steps involved in each pair of shoes his father made, and Hu Weidong had a few questions about each of them. He carried a small, black leather-bound notebook with him to carefully note down all of his father's wisdom. He then took it out again at night, once he had slipped under his duvet, to review every note.

Despite his efforts, Hu Weidong remained an apprentice for five full years before his father let him make his first pair of shoes all by himself. This contributed to Hu Weidong's own perception of his skills as mediocre. He felt that he could only achieve the same accomplishments as others by doubling his efforts. This understanding became the driving force of his apprenticeship. From his first day on the trade, he never let his guard slip. He persevered until he became the face of leather shoes on Xinhe Street.

Throughout it all, Hu Weidong knew that his beginnings did not amount to much, particularly because he felt the depth and complexity of his thoughts were far from those of a successful entrepreneur. Therefore, he made a point of taking the initiative to smile and greet everyone in the company, asking questions whenever he encountered something that he did not understand. He invested a significant amount of time in taking part in grassroots educational activities of all sorts. Some of them were organised by the government, some by student organisations, some by individuals for profit. Some were long, while others were short. Some were of a high level, others were not. This is how Hu Weidong actually made Wang

Wuxian's acquaintance – both attended an Executive MBA group organised by a college association at Xinhe Street. With a two-year curriculum, its studentship was composed of Xinhe Street entrepreneurs and business owners. Hu Weidong was regarded as a person of virtue and prestige and was unanimously elected class president. Meanwhile, Wang Wuxian's character also earned him the favour of his classmates. He was appointed a committee member of the student association and was put in charge of logistics and leisure activities.

When they met each other, Hu Weidong had already heard about the guarantee company industry, although he had not come into contact with it. He simply had no need for their services because banks offered loans to him. He knew nothing about the actual workings of a guarantee company. When he learnt that Wang Wuxian had such a company, he took the initiative to ask him for advice. Needless to say, Wang Wuxian was very honoured to give him a brief but complete introduction to the operations of his guarantee company. Hu Weidong pondered over what he just heard for a little while and then asked Wang Wuxian, 'May I ask you what is your company's annual return rate?'

Extending three fingers, Wang Wuxian replied, 'The lowest one would be 30 per cent. The maximum can reach over 100 per cent. If you were to invest one hundred million in my company, you might recover the principal within one year.'

'Those are quite the windfall profits!'

'What's your company's annual return rate?'

'At its best, not higher than 10 per cent.'

Wang Wuxian leaned against Hu Weidong's shoulder. 'So what leather shoe company are you running?' he asked half in jest. 'Just transfer the funds to my company and don't give another thought to that.'

Hu Weidong stared warily at Wang Wuxian, 'How could I do that?'

Of course, Hu Weidong would not transfer his funds to Wang Wuxian's company. There was one thing he understood: making leather shoes was his occupation, the painstaking efforts of two generations, father and son. Besides, other than making leather shoes, he did not know what else he could do. He had no self-confidence. Last but not least, he had no shortage of money. The bank was even making arrangements to increase his credit line! He worried that it would be more money than he would know what to do with. The way he saw it, the high return rate of the guarantee company was hollow, something that could not possibly bring him the same peace of mind that his trading in the leather shoe industry did. This is how their conversation ended.

The following month, Wang Wuxian took Hu Weidong out for drinks twice a week. Wang Wuxian arranged every boozy get-together, with the majority of his guests being entrepreneurs who ranked first in Xinhe Street, while the rest were leaders from governmental departments. Nobody at the table ever missed a chance to joke about Wang Wuxian's sexual orientation, and he never failed to giggle and show a very merry disposition.

One more month passed and Wang Wuxian popped by Hu Weidong's leather shoe company to 'take a look.' Hu Weidong guided him thoroughly through the entire facility and explained the company's current situation, including its annual sales volume and profitability. Once they were back in Hu Weidong's office, Wang Wuxian gave Hu Weidong a grinning look and asked him, 'So, have you given some thought to that thing I told you about last month?'

Hu Weidong pretended not to understand. 'What thing?' he asked.

'Oh, sure enough, you're an important man and so many things slip your mind. See, I advised you to deposit some money into my guarantee company!'

'Oh, true, I forgot.'

'You could try with a few million first. Soon enough you'll see that the original ways of production are too backward. This will change your view of the world,' Wang Wuxian tried to reassure him.

'Let me give it some more thought.'

'What else is there to think about? Just a few million

to give it a go, it's not like it's going to affect your company in any way.'

'It's not a matter of a few million. I worry that I'll go a step further than that and it'll be difficult to make it back,' explained Hu Weidong.

'Dammit, if you don't see it come back, you don't withdraw it. Look at others who do business. Is there anybody who doesn't make it out whole? Better than before, even.'

Hu Weidong shook his head repeatedly. 'I don't feel at peace with this kind of investment,' he said.

Seeing him talk like that, Wang Wuxian could only shake his head in turn.

Another two months went by, until one day at noon their EMBA class organised a mid-afternoon get-together for drinks. Hu Weidong's driver arrived, and they gave Wang Wuxian a ride back home too. As soon as the car went past Wang Wuxian's guarantee company, he tilted his head and asked Hu Weidong, 'Do you want to come to take a look at my company?'

Hu Weidong saw it was still early and nodded a little. 'OK, I'll just go to learn something.'

Wang Wuxian's guarantee company was located in an office building and could not be seen from the outside. Only a sign on the ground floor lobby indicated that the company was located on the tenth floor. As Wang Wuxian himself explained, the company was not big, only 120 square metres. It had a multipurpose office, two managers' offices and Wang Wuxian's own CEO office.

When the pair got to Wang Wuxian's personal office, he giggled and announced to Hu Weidong, 'I'll show you something.'

'What is it?'

'You'll see.'

Having said that, Wang Wuxian proceeded to lock the office door before opening a cabinet under his bureau desk. Inside there was a safe that he opened as well, taking out a book that he handed over to Hu Weidong. The latter stared at the book and then at Wang Wuxian before asking, 'What is this?'

Wang Wuxian pouted. 'Open it and see!' he said.

Hu Weidong sat down on the chair in front of Wang Wuxian's desk, held the book in his left hand and opened it with his right. His heart jumped abruptly in his chest. He flipped the pages of the book, and as he did, his heartbeat grew stronger, as if an iron hammer was hitting his chest. He was looking at a register of names from whom Wang Wuxian's guarantee company had borrowed funds, one account after another. Next to each entry were written the names of individuals and companies, all with good reputations on Xinhe Street. The longer he flipped through the book, the more important the names written in it were. Many people were his friends – friends who never said a word about having trusted a guarantee company with their funds. Not to mention some of the big names that were listed in the registry! Many of them were bigwigs from Xinhe Street working at all sorts of government departments.

Once he was done looking at the book, Hu Weidong closed it and shut his eyes. He let out a long sigh, and then, opening his eyes again, he asked Wang Wuxian, 'Why are you showing me something this confidential?'

Wang Wuxian giggled and replied, somewhat provocatively, 'I thought I'd let you know just how many people in this city are related to my guarantee company.'

The two of them became suddenly quiet. After a short while, Wang Wuxian laughed again and asked Hu Weidong, 'So how do you feel about it now?'

'I'm a simple man. I fear there's only one thing I know how to do in this life.'

'Well, how will you know if you don't try?'

'Unlike others, I'm pretty thick-skulled,' said Hu Weidong.

'Dammit, I don't buy it!'

However, Wang Wuxian was all talk. He was not going to force Hu Weidong to do anything. Hu Weidong knew it himself too; Wang Wuxian would not take a knife to his throat.

Another month went by, and Hu Weidong got a

call from Wang Wuxian. 'Do you have cash at hand?' asked Wang Wuxian.

'What happened?'

'If you have some, lend it to me. I'll give it back in seven days.'

'How much do you need?' asked Hu Weidong.

'RMB five million.'

Hu Weidong paused for a moment, then replied, 'Give me the account details.'

'Don't rush to make the transfer. I'll go to your company first and give you the loan agreement.'

'It's just a few days' deadline – never mind that!'

'This is the bare minimal procedure. My company also needs to do some bookkeeping,' explained Wang Wuxian.

Hearing this, Hu Weidong no longer insisted. Wang Wuxian made it to his office half an hour later, producing from his bag two copies of a loan agreement. He proceeded to sign them before letting Hu Weidong sign the papers as well. Each of them kept a copy. Once Wang Wuxian left, Hu Weidong instructed his financial department to transfer five million to Wang Wuxian's bank account.

Once the transfer was made, Hu Weidong immediately felt guilty. He feared that the money he had just let slip from his hand would not make it back to him. After all, five million is no small sum. Besides, Wang Wuxian was a mystery to him. They had indeed been classmates for half a year and had been in regular touch with each other, yet he was unable to see clearly just what kind of person Wang Wuxian was. His attire, neither masculine nor feminine, made people suspicious. His speaking mannerisms and expressions were none the clearer. All in all, he just did not seem to be an honest person. Furthermore, Hu Weidong had felt vigilant about Wang Wuxian's guarantee company from the very beginning. It was a realm of hypotheses that could neither be seen nor touched. Still, in the end he had lent money to Wang Wuxian. He found it extremely difficult to turn down requests from others, and Wang Wuxian had already explained that he would give the money back in seven days. Most importantly, he had just received a sum of money as payment from a customer. The company had no shortage of funds. Even if he had really made the worst decision, even if he had indeed squandered those five million on a bad investment, it would not affect the company's usual operations.

On the afternoon of the seventh day that the money was due, Wang Wuxian rushed back to Hu Weidong's office with his copy of the agreement and said to him, 'I already instructed for the money to be transferred back to your company's account.'

Wang Wuxian had barely left when Hu Weidong got a call from his accounting department. They informed him that a sum of money amounting to RMB 5.15 million had been deposited in the company's account that very morning. Hu Weidong called him immediately afterwards. 'Wang Wuxian, you made a mistake – you transferred RMB 150 000 over the loan amount.'

Wang Wuxian's voice came fine and soft through the receptor as he said with a smile, 'I made no mistake. That money is the interest I owed you.'

'Well, I lent you that money, how can it be that it generated an interest?' Hu Weidong paused for a moment. 'Such a high interest, for that matter?' he added.

Wang Wuxian let out a giggle and replied, 'Do you know just how much I get from others by way of interest? It's a dime. This week I earned RMB 500 000 by using your loan and I gave you RMB 150 000 as interest. Don't you think it's yours to take?'

Wang Wuxian changed his tone and exclaimed, 'You can accept that money with peace of mind!'

Pausing for a moment, he also added, 'I will borrow money from you in the future, so don't turn me down. That's it.'

After talking to Wang Wuxian on the phone, Hu Weidong asked the accounting department to enter that sum of money into the account books. Then he sat down in his office chair, lost in deep thought. He looked back on his interactions with Wang Wuxian, recalling all those times that Wang Wuxian had talked to him.

It dawned on him that from the very beginning he had not had a firm resolution to turn down Wang Wuxian's guarantee company. He also came to understand that his heart was not as pure as he had thought it to be; he coveted things other than leather shoe-making.

A week later, Wang Wuxian asked to borrow another ten million from Hu Weidong. He did not say a word and simply gave a transfer order to the accounting department. Of course, they still needed to sign the loan agreement that Wang Wuxian brought to Hu Weidong's office. Wang Wuxian did not betray his trust on this occasion either. On the afternoon of the seventh day, he transferred RMB 10.3 million to Hu Weidong's company account.

After that, their cooperation became increasingly closer. Hu Weidong thought that weekly transfers were fairly cumbersome and ended up doing long-term deposits to Wang Wuxian, who only needed to transfer the monthly interest to Hu Weidong's company account. As time passed, the amount of money that Wang Wuxian borrowed kept increasing – from ten to twenty million, and then to one hundred million, until it reached two hundred million.

By the time Wang Wuxian was borrowing one hundred million, Hu Weidong's company was already struggling to hand out such a large sum of money. Hu Weidong had to make use of the credit that the bank granted him to borrow three hundred million. One hundred went to the company's development as he expanded the facilities and introduced a new assembly line straight from Italy. The remaining two hundred million were put towards Wang Wuxian's guarantee company, earning up to RMB 600 000 by way of monthly interest. According to Hu Weidong's own calculations, the money would double in the span of three years.

Hu Weidong could not have foreseen that the chain on which the guarantee company relied would break, nor could he have expected that Wang Wuxian would flee. He certainly could not have predicted that his bank loan would expire only one week after Wang Wuxian's escape. Hu Weidong had originally intended to call Wang Wuxian to ask him for a transfer of two hundred million. Now that Wang Wuxian had fled, where could he possibly find that much money to repay the bank? There was something else that Hu Weidong could have never anticipated: the bank seemed to know about his involvement with Wang Wuxian. With the rumour of his escape out, the bank's ultimatum to Hu Weidong's company was immediate – he had one week to settle his debt. Should he fail to meet this deadline, the bank would legally seize Hu Weidong's leather shoe company and sell it at public auction. Meanwhile, suppliers took the same course of action simultaneously, demanding that Hu Weidong pay off his debt with them too. This had never happened before. Suppliers had found a goldmine by providing Hu Weidong with raw and processed materials, and had queued to do so! It was impossible for him to pay them in advance. Early on, Hu Weidong's company had stipulated that payment for all suppliers would be settled in the first quarter, and that the company would not get into arrears on the payment date. Never before had a supplier pressed Hu Weidong to pay, and now they were all joining forces to go knock on his door, demanding to see him. Hu Weidong saw nobody. He switched his phone off and went into hiding.

When suppliers realised that Hu Weidong was nowhere to be seen, they flocked to his company, blocked the main door and threatened to take the factory's machinery away if they didn't see their money.

Hu Weidong was now remorseful. Tempted by money, he had betrayed his original intentions and deviated from his path, which ultimately led to his current predicament. *If only he could have a second chance to act differently,* he thought, *how great would that be!* He would devote himself to vigorously developing his leather shoe company, and would not wish for anything else. When, however, has life ever granted a chance for a do-over?

Chen Naixing

Wang Wuxian was actually not the real boss at the One Plus One Guarantee Company, Chen Naixing was. Wang Wuxian's escape to the United States had been his doing.

Chen Naixing owned 95 per cent of the stock of the One Plus One Guarantee Company. However, he had only used Wang Wuxian's name when registering the company. Only Wang Wuxian knew this. What he ignored, however, was that Chen Naixing had a second guarantee company called the Dongfang Guarantee Company. Chen Naixing was equally absent from the Dongfang Guarantee Company. He had hired a professional manager to run the company as the CEO. Chen Naixing operated in the shadows.

Nobody knew a thing about Chen Naixing's wealth, since he never spoke about it to anybody. In addition to these two guarantee companies, Chen Naixing had also invested in real estate, mineral products and cultural investment enterprises. He also had an immigration intermediary company, an investment company in partnership with American citizens, and another enterprise he owned jointly with residents in the United States. Nobody knew just what kind of business his American company was. He diverted plenty of money to the United States through investment companies. Chen Naixing held a United States residence permit. For him, going there was as common an occurrence as visiting a food market.

Wang Wuxian had no residence permit in the United States. His escape had been arranged in a rush through Chen Naixing's immigration intermediary company.

Chen Naixing's wits were sharper than those of Wang Wuxian. On the eve of the first entrepreneur's escape, the glasses factory owner who had borrowed money from the One Plus One Guarantee Company, he warned Wang Wuxian on the phone, 'There might be trouble soon.'

'What kind of trouble?'

'Banks may face restrictions on the money supply. As soon as that happens, their loans will also follow this trend. As soon as banks tighten up on loans, companies will see cracks in their capital chains. If companies fail to see a return on their capital, they will make a reckless move and turn to guarantee companies. However, if banks don't loosen the restrictions on their monetary policy, businesses will be unable to repay the money they borrowed from guarantee companies and will be unable to keep up. Ultimately, our guarantee company will be burdened with this loss.'

Wang Wuxian patted his forehead. 'Dammit, I just loaned twenty million to a glasses factory today,' he said.

'From now on, you must only borrow money, not loan it.'

'Wouldn't that lead to a fatal deficit?' inquired Wang Wuxian.

'You just do as I say.'

Later that night, Chen Naixing met again with Wang Wuxian and asked him, 'Wang Wuxian, would you be willing to immigrate to the United States?'

Wang Wuxian understood what he meant. 'The problem is, what would I do there?' he replied.

'Don't worry about that; I'll arrange everything.'

Wang Wuxian looked at Chen Naixing. 'How much can you give me?' he asked.

'Say a number.'

'How about five million dollars?'

'That's too much. How about three million?' haggled Chen Naixing.

'How long can I live on three million?'

'OK, let's do this – four million. I'll give you two now, and the other half in one month.'

'All right!'

After a short while, Chen Naixing asked Wang

Wuxian, 'How much money have we invested outside the firm?'

'With part of what we loaned back, there's still over three hundred million outside.' Wang Wuxian told him.

'How much is there in the company's account?'

'Not more than two hundred million.'

'Transfer the money right away,' ordered Chen Naixing.

'Where to?'

Chen Naixing gave him the account number of a Sino-US joint venture. Wang Wuxian transferred the money immediately.

The following day, Wang Wuxian followed Chen Naixing's instructions, and, taking the passport the latter had told him to apply for earlier, left for Shanghai with staff from the immigration intermediary company. They stayed there overnight and rushed to apply for his visa the next morning. There was a long queue, but when Wang Wuxian's turn came, he replied to every question as instructed by the immigration intermediary company staff, and passed the procedures smoothly.

One week later, once the news of the glasses factory owner had spread, Chen Naixing called Wang Wuxian. 'There's one thing you need to remember – once you are in the United States, you must not call me, at least not during this time,' he warned.

'Got it.'

Later that night, Wang Wuxian boarded a plane to New York.

Up to that point, Wang Wuxian still knew nothing about Chen Naixing. In all of these years, he had never, ever come to have a clear view of Chen Naixing – he had never even been to his place. All he had heard was that he lived at some fairly big villa that was frequented by beautiful ladies. However, nobody knew the villa's name, nor had anybody seen those beauties. Chen Naixing seldom met with Wang Wuxian and never went to the company's office. If there ever was any kind of issue, he would simply give commands over the phone. If they really needed to meet, they would only do so at some private bar booth or at a park. Wang Wuxian was in the dark as to what kind of person Chen Naixing was.

Wang Wuxian was by no means alone in his impressions – anyone who had ever come in contact with with Chen Naixing felt the same way. This was not surprising, for Chen Naixing himself remained unsure about just what kind of person he was. His life was full of unwelcome contradictions, although he very much enjoyed the advantages they provided him with. Deep in his heart, he wanted to lead a transparent, stable life. Yet his existence was quite the opposite – it was dark and turbulent. He was well aware that this was not the life he wanted, but he was also not willing to give up his way of living. Sometimes he felt inferior; sometimes he exuded self-confidence. Sometimes he was prudent and cautious, other times he acted vigorously and resolutely.

Chen Naixing had once been a reserved, quiet man. That was fifteen years ago, when he was only thirty years old and the head of the credit department at a state-owned bank on Xinhe Street. It was in that very year that Chen Naixing left the bank. Nobody knew why, nor did he tell anybody.

Fresh out of the bank, Chen Naixing worked as a stock broker for a short time. He had kept an eye on the stocks while working at the bank; he opened an account with a small sum and occasionally speculated. Whether he actually earned or lost money in the stock market, nobody knew. One year later, however, he left the brokerage firm as well and went to Shanxi Province, where he invested in minerals for some four years. He largely operated there and in Inner Mongolia and made, as rumour had it, quite a large sum of money. After four years, Chen Naixing left somebody else in charge of the minerals enterprise and made it back to Xinhe Street where he met Wang Wuxian.

Back then, Wang Wuxian had been an accountant for a credit union, where he was in charge of pulling in deposits. Wang Wuxian was introduced to Chen Naixing by acquaintances and had wanted to get him to deposit some money too. It would have never crossed his mind that Chen Naixing would, in fact, pull him out of the credit union to become the CEO of the One Plus One Guarantee Company.

Chen Naixing had a very clear understanding of the future of the company. Just prior to founding the One Plus One Guarantee Company, he told Wang Wuxian that any such business serving as a mere intermediary could only aspire to a slim profit. Windfall profits could only be reaped by a company that could both borrow and lend money while being simultaneously exposed to high risks. The lifespan of such a risky trade would logically be short. With that certainty in mind, he explained to Wang Wuxian, they could not afford to be overcautious and indecisive when handling matters, nor could they worry about personal gains and losses. They had to watch for opportunities, undertake tasks brazenly and steer clear of uncertainty.

Chen Naixing thought Wang Wuxian was as rootless as he was unwitting. The first time that they met, Wang Wuxian made fun of his own body. Chen Naixing thought that an individual that randomly made fun of himself was surely lacking in self-esteem. This was exactly the kind of person that Chen Naixing was looking for. From the very beginning, he made clear to Wang Wuxian that he was to become his shield, and that he would need to leave Xinhe Street if the guarantee company ever came to any trouble. Wang Wuxian immediately accepted these requirements and, in the same breath, put forward his own. He requested an annual salary of RMB two million and 5 per cent of the One Plus One Guarantee Company's shares. Chen Naixing agreed to his requirements just as quickly.

To a certain extent, Chen Naixing was the same kind of person that Wang Wuxian was. They had plenty in common. For instance, both Wang Wuxian and Chen Naixing were single. However, Chen Naixing's status as a bachelor differed greatly from that of Wang Wuxian in one aspect. Neither Wang Wuxian's sexual orientation nor his gender were ever clear. Chen Naixing was not ambiguous on either of those fronts. He had simply never married. Chen Naixing had plenty of women, and he came to know them through his own particular channel, a certain organisation.

Each of his intrigues lasted for only half a year. Prior to establishing a relationship, he had each woman agree to a verbal contract with him. Over the course of those six months, the woman was forbidden to interact with any other heterosexual males. She could freely choose whether to live in Chen Naixing's villa or not. If she indeed chose to stay there, she was allowed to go out for any activity or social engagement. As long as Chen Naixing authorised her, she could even travel. However, she had to abide by a certain item of their agreement – she could not even disclose her address to friends, let alone take them there. Not even pets were allowed. Should she choose to live elsewhere, she had to be on call every hour. There was another important item: once those six months had passed, she was to disappear entirely from Chen Naixing's life. In the event that they casually bumped into one another, they were to pretend that they did not know each other. Within that half a year, Chen Naixing would pay the woman RMB 600 000 in two instalments: the first one on the very day they made their agreement and the second one on the last day of said agreement.

In between each of his six-month-long relationships with women, Chen Naixing would allow himself to rest for a little over a month. During that time, he would receive a great deal of calls from women who were interested in entering this arrangement with him. They were all outstanding women; this much was evident from listening to them on the phone. On this point, Chen Naixing had peace of mind. He had been turning to the services of this organisation for many years already and the ladies they had on offer always underwent a most rigorous selection process in regards to their skin, their facial features, their figure, their voice and their attitude towards customers. Their requirements concerning their academic qualifications were equally strict. During his month of rest, however,

Chen Naixing wanted to be alone – to be calm and live in quiet. There were certain matters that one could only face alone. He also needed this time to sort out his thoughts. Everybody is bound to accumulate a miscellanea of emotional needs and physical desires in their bodies every once in a while, and so everybody needs to find a chance to clean up. Pent-up issues are sure to impact health and possibly even heavily impact life. It was once Chen Naixing had cleaned out his body of all sorts of rubbish that his mind could reach clarity. It was only then that he could regain the passion to return to the battlefield and readily let a new woman in his life.

No matter who the chosen woman was, Chen Naixing was always honest and nice to her. He always talked to her like this, 'For the next six months, you are the lady of the house here. If there's anything you have to say about me, don't hesitate to do so. I'll do my best to change,' he would say. 'If you're not happy, I can't be happy either,' he would also add. Not only did Chen Naixing speak like that, he played the part as well. He was extremely courteous to every woman that stayed at the villa. His voice was always mild and he had a perennial smile floating on his face. He would always ask for the woman's advice prior to doing anything. If she was in the villa, he would always try to spend time with her. Once the six months came to an end, however, he was adamant about terminating their agreement. There had been women who asked him to extend it for another half a year, but Chen Naixing never considered it and his answer remained unchanged. *No, that was not possible.*

However, when the time came for women to leave the villa, Chen Naixing would always experience a feeling of emptiness in his heart. He would look at the woman's back as she left and feel that both his body and soul were falling. He would remind himself that he was a sinful man in deep need of redemption.

Chen Naixing had come to this realisation over a decade ago. His awareness only grew more acute upon founding his guarantee companies. He felt rather desperate sometimes. He lay on his villa's sofa and the whole house spun as he increasingly shrank, until he was so tiny he could not breathe. That feeling struck him every time he earned a large sum of money through interest payments, and it grew stronger each time.

On one such occasion, he did not dare stay in his villa nor even on Xinhe Street. He found himself driving at high speed without a fixed destination and winding up in Zhoushan Prefecture. Since he was there already, he thought, *I might as well go to Mount Putuo*. Once there, he followed the masses until he made it to Yangzhi Guanyin Stele, where the incense was so intense that the smoke made it difficult for visitors to open their eyes. Chen Naixing found a wooden seat and sat far away, watching temple-goers burn incense and then kneel to kowtow endlessly. He did not know how long he had watched the flood of people dispersing slowly before eventually standing and walking up to the door of the Buddhist temple himself. He looked up at Guanyin Bodhisattva and found that she too was looking down on him. He felt his mind quiver, as though a tray of ice water had been poured over his head. His entire body trembled and his legs involuntarily made him kneel on the woven cattail hassock. He bowed his head and kowtowed. All of a sudden, his heart calmed down, as if a large door had opened and out toppled all his inner debris, experiencing a feeling of void after this encounter.

Chen Naixing then entered the main hall of the temple and saw that it hosted a glass statuette of Guanyin to be venerated by visitors. The small sculpture was also looking at him and he felt his mind shiver again. He immediately sought the temple's abbot to see whether he could place an offering that would buy him the glass statuette. The abbot was actually pleased to accommodate his petition, and so Chen Naixing asked him, 'How much money would that be?'

The abbot laughed and replied, 'As much as you think it's worth.'

Chen Naixing opened his purse, where he carried

over RMB twenty thousand in cash. He took the money out and placed it on the incense case. Holding Guanyin, he left – walking on tiptoes.

After returning to Xinhe Street, Chen Naixing placed the Guanyin statuette in the attic of his villa and made sure to burn incense for her daily. He came to realise that his heart felt the calmest at those moments. From then on, he went to the attic every time there was turmoil in his heart. As long as he stayed there for a while, he could slowly forget everything that went on outside.

The attic was the only locked room in the villa. Chen Naixing warned the women who came to his villa not to go there. *What did the attic hide?* Their questions only managed to make him double down on his warning. Every time he went to the attic, he locked himself in from the inside. Nobody else was to enter.

In addition to his veneration of the Guanyin Bodhisattva statuette, Chen Naixing later took to another regular ritual. Every year he sponsored ten impoverished children to go to school. All the children were in private contact with the local education bureau, which produced a list of names for Chen Naixing. He would go to the school to personally check and select the students, promising each of them that their studies would be funded up until their college graduation.

After arranging for Wang Wuxian's escape, Chen Naixing ran into the attic, burned an incense stick for

Guanyin Bodhisattva and kneeled on the cattail hassock. Hu Weidong's shadow dwelled constantly on his
mind. He was worried that Hu Weidong would not be
able to stand the blow and that a major tragedy would
occur. His mind would never find peace again if that
ever happened. Chen Naixing burned that incense stick
for Hu Weidong.

Jiang Lina

After Hu Weidong went into hiding, he handed over the shambles of the Zhenxing Leather Shoe Company to his wife, Jiang Lina. There were people on Xinhe Street who cursed Hu Weidong, claiming that the son of a bitch had vanished in the face of trouble, leaving his wife behind to cover up the whole mess.

In fact, it was Jiang Lina who plotted Hu Weidong's hiding. This is how she analysed everything for Hu Weidong's attentive ears. 'You are too big of a target right now; you are the main firing point. If you're at the company, all eyes will be on you. Your every word, anything you do will be magnified by a hundred. However, you cannot afford to remain silent or inactive in your current situation. You just cannot. If you don't say a word, if you don't do anything, people will certainly say that you're running away. What can you possibly say right now, though? What can you possibly do? The first thing you ought to do is take the money out and pay it back to the

bank and your suppliers. You are not in a position to do that right now. It is what it is, so your safest choice is to step out of the spotlight for a while.'

Hu Weidong listened to her and thought she was right, but he could not put his mind at ease. 'What will you do once I'm gone?' he asked Jiang Lina.

'I'm the weaker sex. What are they going to do to me?' she replied.

'That's really not right; let's get away together!'

Jiang Lina thought that what Hu Weidong really meant by 'getting away' was running away, that he wanted to follow the steps of other businessmen at Xinhe Street who had wrapped up their capital and fled to begin anew. Jiang Lina knew that these were not easy words for Hu Weidong. She was aware that he must have thought it all over and over before concluding that there really was no other way. It did not escape Jiang Lina that for Hu Weidong to really consider giving up Zhenxing Leather Shoe Company, he must have truly felt there was not a thread of hope to cling to. Otherwise, Hu Weidong would have not surrendered.

Zhenxing Leather Shoe Company always came first in Hu Weidong's mind. He would have never done anything that could be harmful to the firm. That was why he had been slow to react when faced with Wang Wuxian's constant solicitations; he was afraid that any potential incident would end up compromising the

company's regular operation. It had been Jiang Lina's decision to finally give Wang Wuxian the money. Jiang Lina had said that while he only ever saw the pessimistic side of everything, things invariably had an optimistic side as well. Any money made from this loan-sharking operation could be put towards expanding the leather shoe company's production scale. Needless to say, Jiang Lina couldn't have imagined that Wang Wuxian would ultimately flee and that their money would be drained away. However, that was not to say that Jiang Lina agreed with Hu Weidong's idea of escaping. In her mind, running away was tantamount to admitting defeat, raising their own hands in capitulation and doing away with themselves. This was all foreign to Jiang Lina's nature. Jiang Lina made a few calculations for Hu Weidong. The current debt of Zhenxing Leather Shoe Company was up to an estimated RMB five hundred million, with three hundred million due to the bank and with approximately two hundred million remaining. She had also calculated the assets of Zhenxing Leather Shoe Company, which amounted to at least RMB seven hundred million, including some outstanding payment for goods. Moreover, the company still had a contingency fund.

She said to Hu Weidong, 'Zhenxing Leather Shoe Company isn't facing insolvency or any situation it cannot control. The company is only temporarily unable to settle the bank loan and the payment due to suppliers. As long as we can locate the necessary funds to pay off the bank loan, all other issues will be readily solved. Where is the need to escape, then? Is that necessary at all?'

'Of course I know the company isn't insolvent just yet, but where are we going to find three hundred million to settle the debt with the bank?' replied Hu Weidong.

'You don't have to worry about that, just leave it to me. Worry about finding a place to go into hiding for a while. If you stay here, you'll only manage to make things worse. You'll come out once I have settled everything.'

Hu Weidong listened to Jiang Lina and did not argue. He knew Jiang Lina was a capable woman with ideas of her own. He had become well aware of that when he first fell in love with her, and it was a trait of hers that he liked. That being said, he was doubtful that Jiang Lina would indeed be able to find three hundred million to borrow. Had the leather shoe company been operating under normal circumstances, borrowing one billion would have been very possible, yet this was a most particular time, full of turmoil and chaos. *People will keep dodging you — who on earth is going to lend you the money?* However, seeing Jiang Lina's confidence, but also seeing he really had no other solution, Hu Weidong had to pack a few changes of clothing and secretly leave for a distant relative's place in the countryside. This relative was Hu Weidong's mother's older cousin, whom he called uncle. As a child, Hu Weidong accompanied his mother to visit him every year during the Spring Festival. Hu Weidong's uncle lived on a big mountain in the famous Nanxi River scenic area. His was the only household for five kilometres around – not a soul would bother him there. After his mother's passing, Hu Weidong kept visiting his uncle every Spring Festival, or Chinese New Year, bringing with him some daily necessities and RMB two thousand as seasonal gifts. Nobody knew of this relative of his, which meant Hu Weidong would be safe there.

Once she saw Hu Weidong off, Jiang Lina got down to business immediately. *There was no other way to go about things!* The bank loan deadline had come already, and everything would be over the minute the courts intervened. Therefore, Jiang Lina's first step was to locate the bank president. Once she did, she presented the situation in the following way, 'If your bank decides to enter legal procedures and make the courts proceed to auction the company, it'll still mean a loss for the bank, even if you get the three hundred million back. Not only would you fail to get any interest payments, you would also lose an important customer.'

'Let me see, what are your plans?' said the bank president.

'Give me half a month and I'll bring you the stipulated three hundred million plus the interest.'

'What guarantee can you offer that you will indeed do so?' continued the president.

'I cannot give you one hundred per cent guarantee, but I am confident that I'll find a way. Besides, giving me a chance will be beneficial for both our business and your bank. If our company manages to be reborn from its ashes, your bank will also be reaping the profits and enhancing your reputation.'

'Half a month is too long – I won't be able to justify it to the top. Seven days is all I can give you.'

Jiang Lina replied to his words, 'Fair enough, seven days, but I have a condition.'

'What condition?'

'Once I settle our debt with you and we apply for a new loan, I would like to get your endorsement. Without it, all this would be in vain.'

The bank's president smiled at her and said, 'I had heard before how terrific you are, and you've certainly lived up to my expectations today. Since you've been honest with me, I will also be honest with you. You can count on my endorsement should you apply for a new loan. However, you should also know that the way things stand at Xinhe Street right now, my word will not count as final for a loan like yours. That decision rests with the head office.'

'Thank you, sir. Having your word on this matter reassures me.'

Once she got the seven days' extension from the bank, Jiang Lina did not rush to try and find the money. Instead, she convened a meeting with the company's middle managers, followed by another with the entire factory's staff. Clearly and concisely, she briefed everyone on the company's issues. The company, she told the workers, was indeed facing some difficulties. However, Hu Weidong had already set out to raise funds. He would be back in a few days, and once he was, the company's usual operation would be quickly resumed. They needed to trust the company. Moreover, Jiang Lina announced, all workers would receive – effective immediately – a month's wages, to be calculated according to the salary they had received last month.

The staff welcomed Jiang Lina's words with shouts of approval as their applause flooded the assembly hall. Jiang Lina let out a sigh of relief. She knew very well that appeasing and stabilising the company's workers was the most urgent matter. She worried about their spirits the most. Staying in the dark about the company's current state of affairs would have merely rendered them vulnerable to believe any rumours. Wages were the workers' main concern. Had they worked hard for the month only to have their boss run away and the company collapse? Who would pay them their salaries? In such a situation, and lacking faith in the company, they would have failed to turn up to work. Once the company's machinery had been removed, one worker leading the charge could cause the rest of the staff to follow suit. If the workers scattered, the company would never recover. Therefore, no matter what, no efforts could be spared in keeping the staff. As long as the workers kept working regularly, the leather shoe company would be able to maintain its usual production as well, and its basic operation would remain undisturbed. This would, by comparison, make all other issues seem minor. As for the suppliers who had come to besiege the factory, they would tactfully back away as soon as they saw orderly workers clocking in every day. Their worries were similar to those of the staff, and now that things were on the mend with the company performing as per usual, they would understand that their payment was secure and nobody would feel the need to openly quarrel with the company. After all, they would get nothing good out of the company's collapse. On the contrary, if the company proceeded with its regular rhythm, they would be sure to return for some good business!

With those two issues out of her way, Jiang Lina shifted her focus back to settling the bank loan. Where to find the money? Jiang Lina thought of Chen Naixing.

She had her reasons. They used to be colleagues at the credit union, back when Chen Naixing was the head of the credit department and she was his subordinate. He had cared for her greatly and was a very attentive, mindful person – to everyone. Whenever his subordinates made mistakes, he never pointed them out, but rather redid everything himself. Even so, Jiang Lina had vaguely perceived that Chen Naixing cared about her a bit more than he did about the rest of their colleagues. He entrusted her with all-important tasks. This made Jiang Lina develop a certain trust towards him. Warmth flooded her whenever he came to her mind and whenever she saw him. Jiang Lina never felt that she was particularly outstanding among her colleagues. If she had any strengths in comparison to others, it would be her resilience, her initiative and her frankness.

There was another reason for her gratitude towards Chen Naixing. Thanks to him, she met Hu Weidong, who had come over to their credit union to apply for a loan. Back then, Hu Weidong's company had just started to expand. When he went to their bank to ask for a loan, Chen Naixing let Jiang Lina take care of his business. It was Jiang Lina who made the most of this convenient chance to take the initiative and ask Hu Weidong out for dinner. Hu Weidong had hoped to come back from the bank with pockets full of money, so he did not dare turn her down. Plus, he did not have much experience back then. Since he was a child, leather shoe-making was all he knew. Previously, he had only interacted with people from the lowest classes of society. He regarded Jiang Lina as a person who held an iron rice bowl; he thought of her as having a secure job, crisp and clean looks, and fingers resembling tender ginger shoots. She also had a certain mysterious fragrance. He did not even dare to look her in the eye. That alone was already enough to make him shrink to half of his frame.

When Jiang Lina asked him out, he assumed that she wanted to discuss the loan and did not dare to elaborate. When Jiang Lina saw Hu Weidong's shy disposition, it added to the reasons she liked him. She liked Hu Weidong's simplicity, even if it made him look a bit common. Jiang Lina felt he was reliable precisely because of his simplicity. In her mind, men like that were easy to control. Men like that would not do anything improper. There was something else that felt crucial, and that Jiang Lina came to see by contacting Hu Weidong and inspecting his leather shoe company – he had a fine future ahead of him. He had the skills to make leather shoes, he was experienced in managing his staff and he had earned a reputation for himself over the course of a decade. Most importantly, Jiang Lina valued Hu Weidong's dependability and the solid way in which he did everything, one step at a time. With her help, Hu Weidong could launch his own career. *How could she let a man like that go?*

Therefore, Jiang Lina went on the offensive and

asked Hu Weidong out for dinner. Later, she also made the first move to grab Hu Weidong's hand. When she pulled his hand into hers, she noticed that it was stiff, and that his first reaction had been to retract it altogether. Jiang Lina, however, felt joyful. She looked attentively at Hu Weidong's hands. They were sturdy, solid and calloused – the fruit of his leather shoe-making experience, the very embodiment of labour. Jiang Lina was pleased to see that Hu Weidong's hands were also immaculate. His fingernails were neatly trimmed and without a trace of dirt. This proved that he was a clean-living, honest man. Jiang Lina had been to his workplace, full of black dirt and a pungent smell that assailed the nostrils. Neither affected Hu Weidong's appearance. Jiang Lina could perceive a particular scent emanating from him, which one she could not tell – but she liked it. When she sensed that smell, her body went limp, as if her bones were softening and she felt gradually fatigued. Again, it was Jiang Lina who labelled the bond between them as a relationship. She did not really state it verbally. Jiang Lina did not say a word and neither did Hu Weidong. She charmed Hu Weidong into kissing her. When he did, he hugged her against his chest anxiously, asking repeatedly, *Is this true? Is this real?*

'Why, of course, it is,' replied Jiang Lina. It was at her place that Jiang Lina gave her virginity to Hu

Weidong, by her own initiative as well. The whole time, Hu Weidong asked, *May I? May I?* The following day, Hu Weidong's family presented Jiang Lina's with the appropriate betrothal gifts.

After their wedding, Jiang Lina kept working at the bank for a while. Her position there meant that Hu Weidong's loans were dealt with much more smoothly. Out of vanity, in a way, Hu Weidong had hoped she would stay there. It was a matter of pride to have a wife who worked at a bank, wearing a uniform daily. He had also wished for Jiang Lina to remain independent after they married. Working at the bank, she would have a significant salary, her own life and her own sizeable space. Moreover, if Jiang Lina were to resign from her job to work at his company, her talent would be somewhat lost at an insignificant position. Hu Weidong's company already had professional financial staff. Jiang Lina's occasional help to Hu Weidong in her free time was more than enough.

In the end, Jiang Lina resigned from her job five years into their marriage. At that time, Hu Weidong's Zhenxing Leather Shoe Company had already become a steadily rising star on Xinhe Street. The company had moved to new facilities and the staff had also gone from a hundred people to over a thousand. Hu Weidong's shortcomings were now visible. He only had his vocational training and lacked education. This had not posed any problem when he only had a hundred employees and his skills were persuasive enough. However, once the staff reached a thousand workers, administrating them and managing the company became increasingly complicated, and his skillset was no longer enough. Furthermore, financial matters had expanded with the company. It would have been very easy for the company's operation to quickly become unbalanced, having to deal with huge figures and with Hu Weidong's focus still on the technical side of the business. Once Jiang Lina became aware of this, she resigned from her position at the bank without hesitation.

At that time, she was already the credit department's chief official, but she knew that Hu Weidong needed her more. She knew her priorities.

Once she began working for the Zhenxing Leather Shoe Company, she truly took to her role as the boss' wife, supervising the company's management, finances and sales. Hu Weidong could focus on the technical side of the business and come up with new products. Furthermore, Jiang Lina did her best to ensure that Hu Weidong had plenty of opportunities to engage in educational activities. Those would simultaneously allow him to work on his self-improvement and meet other students, people who could be helpful in promoting the factory's future development.

Hu Weidong trusted Jiang Lina implicitly and

did not object to her resignation from the bank. His own horizons had been broadened by the company's development over the last five years. He no longer glorified his wife's position at the bank, nor did he have to apply for bank loans any more. Instead, the banks sought him out, hoping that he would borrow a larger amount of funds from them. It went without saying that the bank had its own interests at heart and wanted Hu Weidong to open his main account there, so that the company's funds would be deposited at the bank. Hu Weidong handed over all of the financial matters to Jiang Lina. While he became the chairman, the company's actual lifeline depended on her.

After Jiang Lina's wedding, Chen Naixing resigned from the bank due to his feelings for her. She gave Chen Naixing a small present on the occasion of her engagement, since he was the reason she had met Hu Weidong in the first place. Chen Naixing attended their wedding, but was not in the bank when she went back to work. Eventually, she heard from a colleague that Chen Naixing had left two weeks after her wedding.

Jiang Lina heard the news and felt a deep sense of loss. She thought about her time at the bank and as she did, Chen Naixing's figure appeared distinctly right before her eyes. After all, he had been her matchmaker! Now she had no chance to express her gratitude. Besides, Jiang Lina had a faint impression that Chen Naixing's resignation was somehow related to her, even if she couldn't say how.

After Chen Naixing resigned, Jiang Lina always paid attention to news about him. She heard plenty of tales about him and his many mysterious investments. She heard that he was a stealthy, rich and powerful man whose fortune remained unknown to all. In short, he was Xinhe Street's most cryptic enigma, a man that nobody could claim to really know. Every time someone mentioned Chen Naixing, his figure sprang to Jiang Lina's mind, and she realised that her sense of trust in him remained intact. Whenever she thought of him, she felt something warm inside. Therefore, when Hu Weidong saw himself in trouble because of his usury, she immediately thought of turning to Chen Naixing for help. She firmly believed that Chen Naixing would reach out and help her as long as it was in his power. She was also convinced that he had that power indeed.

Even though Jiang Lina had not contacted Chen Naixing over the last ten years, she had always kept his mobile phone number. Had it not been because of Hu Weidong's company coming into trouble due to local loan-sharking, she would have probably never called Chen Naixing. Things, however, had now come to a crisis. Chen Naixing was the only one who could help her.

Jiang Lina found Chen Naixing's number in her phone's contacts, took a breath, and dialled it. The characteristic beep on the other side indicated that the receiver had yet to pick up the call. Jiang Lina paused for a moment. She could not know for certain whether Chen Naixing still used that phone number, but it was a miracle that it was still in service after ten years. When no one picked up, Jiang Lina hung up and redialled a moment later. The phone call went through again, and again it went unanswered. Jiang Lina hung up and waited some fifteen minutes – fifteen minutes that seemed interminable, so much so that Jiang Lina felt she could hear seconds ticking, with abysmal gaps between each one. It was only when Jiang Lina called a third time that a voice replied at the other end of the line.

'Hello?'

Jiang Lina knew Chen Naixing's voice as soon as she heard it. That was his voice indeed; it had not changed one bit. Her heart warmed up and she replied, 'This is Jiang Lina.'

'Hello,' said Chen Naixing.

'My leather shoe company has some cash flow issues. I need your help.'

'Fine.'

'Can we meet for a moment?'

'I'm not on Xinhe Street. Tell me about it first! What kind of help do you need?' asked the voice on the line.

'I need to borrow money from you.'

'How much?'

'Four hundred million,' Jiang Lina said confidently.

'Is this because of some bad loans?'

'Yes.'

Chen Naixing muttered to himself, then said, 'That figure's a bit high, may I give you an answer tomorrow?'

'Of course.'

Jiang Lina was stunned for a good while after hanging up. Her heart felt cold. She could feel that Chen Naixing had not told the truth. Listening to the sounds at the other end of the line, she could tell that he actually was on Xinhe Street. Furthermore, he had turned down her plea to meet him. She felt that this refusal was fairly telling and that his excuses meant that he was choosing to avoid her. *As for the delay in his answer, that was also most likely an excuse!* However, Jiang Lina could not confirm her own suspicions. After all, based on her own understanding of Chen Naixing, he was not that kind of person. Seldom had he said a word, but when he did open his mouth, he had been honest. He had never spoken ambiguously, nor did he ever make empty promises.

Jiang Lina couldn't figure out what was on Chen Naixing's mind. Back in the day, when she worked with Chen Naixing, she had never had the opportunity to truly see his personality in this light. If there was something that needed to be addressed, she simply opened her mouth, talked to Chen Naixing and promptly forgot it all. She never noticed his reaction. Whenever she heard their colleagues talk about Chen Naixing as an inscrutable, astute individual, she never had any immediate feelings towards their assessment and thought it was none of her business. Later on, she would come to hear plenty of gossip, none of which she ever paid any attention to. Rather, she would simply think, *You all are sweating it way too much!* Now, however, she was experiencing it all first-hand. She really could not think of any other solution, though. Where else could she possibly find four hundred million? All she could do was wait for Chen Naixing's answer and hope that her own perception of him would not betray her – that Chen Naixing was the same man she had trusted in the past. In her heart, she resolved to accept whichever harsh conditions Chen Naixing might impose to help her overcome this time of hardship. After all, four hundred million was indeed a large sum.

The following day at noon, Chen Naixing called her back, as expected, and agreed to lend her three hundred million. Even though this amount was still far from the four hundred million Jiang Lina needed, she was deeply moved by his gesture. *A friend in need was a friend indeed!* After Hu Weidong lost favour, ten of his former sworn brothers, his faithful friends, had all been dodging them. Most of these people were also in the leather shoe trade, and all of them were big shots with hundreds of millions. In the face of trouble, Jiang Lina had set up a rescue plan for the company with Hu Weidong. She hoped to borrow a sum of money from each of his ten sworn brothers to settle the bank loan first. However, by the time Hu Weidong walked away, those who did not go into hiding themselves argued that their own funds had been absorbed by the guarantee company. Hu Weidong was very discouraged by this.

Jiang Lina herself couldn't really blame Hu Weidong's sworn brothers. After all, they had also been affected by the guarantee company. All of them had taken loans from the bank, which was undoubtedly urging them to settle their debts. They were in the same predicament. Considering their situation, Chen Naixing's actions were even more valuable in comparison. When she heard his call, Jiang Lina felt warmth seeping through her insides, as well as the urge to cry. She held the phone and said, 'I will pay you back as soon as possible; I really will.'

However, Jiang Lina could not have anticipated Chen Naixing's reply. 'I don't want you to pay me back. I'm giving you this money on one condition.'

'What condition? Say it!'

'I want 49 per cent of your leather shoe company's shares.'

His words left Jiang Lina dumbfounded. She had not expected Chen Naixing to impose such a condition. *Wasn't he making firewood out of the fallen tree? Why on earth did he want 49 per cent of the leather shoe company's shares?* Jiang Lina did not understand. She paused for a moment and then replied, 'That is not up to me to decide. I must bring it up with Hu Weidong.'

'Fair enough, you have two days to consider it. Come back to me once you've made a decision.'

'I will do so as soon as possible.'

'There's something else that I want to make clear beforehand. If you do agree to transfer 49 per cent of your company's shares to me, I will have somebody become the company's chief financial officer. You must keep this in mind before you make a decision,' added Chen Naixing.

It was then that Chen Naixing's ferocity finally dawned on Jiang Lina. He could seize the company's key department without even blinking. As soon as he had one of his people become the chief financial officer, he would not need to dispatch anybody else. He would be well informed on every matter related to the firm. Jiang Lina nodded and said, 'Fine, we will discuss this immediately. I will contact you again as soon as possible.'

Jiang Lina hung up and began to pack to go find Hu Weidong at his hiding place in the Nanxi River mountains. She wouldn't have cell phone service there, nor would she be able to make calls. Luckily enough, Hu Weidong had drawn a map for her before departing. She had only to follow it to locate Hu Weidong. She could not make a decision about Chen Naixing's terms on her own. Accepting his conditions was equal to selling the company. She needed to bring this up with Hu Weidong.

Just as Jiang Lina was about to set off, Hu Weidong appeared right in front of her. Jiang Lina was taken aback. She could not believe her own eyes. She blinked, shook her head, and looked at him again. It was Hu Weidong all right. She blurted out, 'How come you're back?'

'I couldn't stop worrying about you,' Hu Weidong replied.

When Jiang Lina heard this, she burst into tears and she turned her head away deliberately. Once she had calmed down, she told him about Chen Naixing. Hu Weidong remained silent for a long while afterwards. Eventually, as though speaking to himself, he said, 'It's all my fault. All of it.'

Jiang Lina noticed that his eyes were red and his lips were twitching involuntarily. She knew what Hu Weidong felt. He had single-handedly developed his leather shoe factory. They were childless – or rather, the factory was their only child. Now they were going to hand half of that child over to someone else. *Who wouldn't be heartbroken?* With this in mind, Jiang Lina reached for Hu Weidong's hands to hold in hers and softly said, 'We would retain the company no matter what, and there would be more opportunities in the future. Besides, we would have 51 per cent of the company's shares and we would be the main shareholders.'

Hu Weidong took her hands to hold them tightly. He nodded.

Ai Mengya

Ai Mengya was the person Chen Naixing had designated as the financial director of the Zhenxing Leather Shoe Company. Prior to that, she had also been the boss of the Dongfang Guarantee Company. Much like Wang Wuxian, Ai Mengya was hired by Chen Naixing. Unlike Wang Wuxian, however, Ai Mengya's Dongfang Guarantee Company dealt mostly with car insurance and did not involve usury. Up to that point, the Dongfang Guarantee Company made up 70 per cent of the car insurance business on Xinhe Street. This percentage alone generated over RMB twenty million worth of annual profits. This, along with their other business, meant the Dongfang Guarantee Company generated an annual net profit of approximately RMB thirty million. It was Chen Naixing's most stable investment.

Ai Mengya had also been Chen Naixing's former subordinate. She had joined the bank's credit section two years after Jiang Lina. Just a year after that, Chen Naixing resigned and left his post.

Ai Mengya had been an auditing major and had joined the bank after graduation. She was thin and willowy – even her chest seemed rather flat. Her eyes, nose and mouth were just as fine as her soft voice. Her skin was covered by a thin layer of golden fluff, as though she had yet to fully develop! Her colleagues at the credit section were somewhat disappointed.

At work, Ai Mengya only did what she was told. Whatever task Chen Naixing gave her, she completed it fully, but in a way that was hard to detect any of her downfalls or capabilities. Pressed to highlight any distinctive trait about her, one might have mentioned the way she spoke. Each of her sentences was short and comprised merely a few words, as though they were rough drafts of conversation. There was also her orderly way of dealing with any matter – whenever a customer came to apply for a loan, she used the simplest language to clearly explain the process involved, fully detailing the application procedures, as well as the materials the client needed to submit. The loan applications she handled were the neatest and most standardised in terms of information provided and filled out. Most customers did not need to come back to the bank a second time to fix mistakes.

At the credit department, Chen Naixing and Ai

agree to that. They asked her why not, but she never gave them a reason. She seemed as though she was waiting for something – but what it was, she did not know. She did not want to leave her post at the Audit Office and had planned to remain there until her retirement.

In her ninth year, she received a phone call from Chen Naixing. He wanted her to become the boss of the Dongfang Guarantee Company. Once she heard his voice, she agreed immediately.

She stayed at the Dongfang Guarantee Company for a little over two years. Prior to her joining the company, the car insurance market on Xinhe Street had been basically non-existent. She built up the business all by herself. If a car was on the roads, Ai Mengya had already handled its insurance. However, just when the business was flourishing, Chen Naixing called on her to become the chief financial officer of the Zhenxing Leather Shoe Factory. She was initially unwilling to accept his offer, and she asked him, 'What about the Dongfang Guarantee Company?'

'You'll be in charge of both places simultaneously,' Chen Naixing told her.

'I am worried that I won't do well.'

'I trust your ability,' Chen Naixing replied. 'I wouldn't trust anybody else.'

Ai Mengya heard his reassurance and said nothing else.

Ai Mengya had her reasons for not wanting to go to Zhenxing Leather Shoe Company. She did not want to see Jiang Lina. Back in her days of working at the bank's credit department, Jiang Lina had cared about her. Ai Mengya usually remained silent and did not seem to be a very friendly person. Jiang Lina had always taken the initiative to invite her to whatever activity was happening in the department, whether it be going out for her break at noon or for dinner in the evening. Ai Mengya invariably smiled as soon as she heard her proposals, sometimes joining in and sometimes opting out.

Still, for some reason that she ignored, Ai Mengya had felt a certain sense of resistance towards Jiang Lina. She could not tell where this feeling came from. There was also another important reason for her to feel reluctant to return to the Zhenxing Leather Shoe Company, as she would be in a bit of an awkward position at the firm this time around. To some extent, her duty there as a chief financial officer would be to supervise things. That was not an honourable role. Besides, Jiang Lina's company was undergoing a major disaster. Even though Jiang Lina had endured it so far, she must have felt bitter about it, and Ai Mengya's arrival was not going to bring her any consolation. This made Ai Mengya feel very uncomfortable.

Ai Mengya's arrival took Jiang Lina by surprise. She saw her at her office as the company's general manager.

Ai Mengya knocked on the door before going in and Jiang Lina did not recognise her at first when she looked up. She lowered her head and went back to writing, only to immediately lift it again and stand up from her office chair. Pointing at Ai Mengya with her right index finger, she said, 'Oh my, aren't you Ai Mengya?'

'I am,' Ai Mengya replied.

Jiang Lina quickly approached her, saying, 'You've put on a little weight and look charming, I didn't recognise you.'

As she spoke, she grabbed Ai Mengya's hand, embraced her shoulder with her free hand and shouted out the door, 'Hu Weidong, come here, quick!'

Hu Weidong didn't know what was going on and trotted to Jiang Lina's office. There he found Jiang Lina, pointing at Ai Mengya as she said to him, 'This is Ai Mengya, our company's newly appointed chief financial officer. She's a former colleague from my days at the bank's credit department and was an outstanding student at university.'

Hu Weidong nodded. 'Hello. Please keep an eye on everything for us,' he said to Ai Mengya.

'I'm causing trouble here,' Ai Mengya replied to Hu Weidong.

Hu Weidong rubbed his hands. 'Just let me know if there's anything that needs to be handled, and I will take care of it,' he said.

Even though this was the first time they met, Ai Mengya felt that Jiang Lina and Hu Weidong both had quite a good mindset. They showed no signs of being defeated, and the company was not in a chaotic situation. This was something that Ai Mengya kept noticing as she continued doing her job.

Chen Naixing had instructed Ai Mengya to check the company's accounts. By giving this order, he had also failed to understand that as a former auditor, and now chief financial officer, Ai Mengya would have done those two things anyway. Jiang Lina had also been a banker and obviously knew what the new financial director would require. Jiang Lina had arranged in advance for the accounts needed by Ai Mengya to be checked and moved to her office.

Ai Mengya first proceeded to check the bank account and the company's books in detail. Then, she checked the company's income and inventory. She went to the warehouse to check whether the industrial production procedure was complying to standards. She also performed a sample check of the stubs that accounted for the company's economic business, inspecting their transaction summary records and the rationality of expenditure. Ai Mengya sighed while verifying everything. Jiang Lina had truly proven herself as the banker she had once been. All the accounts were clear and transparent, including the previous cost accounting as well as the profit calculation. Everything was unequivocal, and the transaction summary records on the company's stubs had also been duly and thoroughly written.

Hu Weidong left the deepest impression on her. Every time they bumped into each other, he always smiled shyly, and his smile was full of regret. He almost always stayed in the workshop and his eyes popped out whenever anyone entered the room in a hurry. Every time she saw him, Ai Mengya felt the urge to say something comforting, but she wasn't quite sure what to say.

To Ai Mengya's professional eye, it was clear from the accounts that Jiang Lina and Hu Weidong were doing serious business. When she went to the warehouse to check the inventory there, she found that it was a clean space where all raw materials and supplies were kept in perfect order. Only someone serious about their business would do things so thoroughly.

Once the verification of the company's state of affairs was complete, Ai Mengya called Chen Naixing to report back on the results and her own impressions. She rarely ever called him, and did so only if she had something special to say. Chen Naixing's calls to her were even rarer – an average of one a month! They met even less than that, sometimes not even once in half a year. Ai Mengya had no idea of Chen Naixing's whereabouts, nor had she any inkling of his activities.

During one of her report calls, Chen Naixing asked her when the Zhenxing Leather Shoe Company would start generating profits. Ai Mengya hesitated and said it was still hard to know. He did not ask again.

Jiang Lina and Hu Weidong did not treat Ai Mengya like an outsider; rather, they invited her to all the company meetings. It was through those meetings Ai Mengya came to realise that after the loan-sharking storm, both Hu Weidong and Jiang Lina had indeed regained their spirits and devoted themselves wholeheartedly to bringing Zhenxing Leather Shoe Company back to normal. They had even developed a hundred-year scheme that included brand-building, talent development, marketing, employee training and so on. However, Ai Mengya also quickly realised that the state of affairs at Zhenxing Leather Shoe Company was pretty far from optimistic. She boiled it down to at least five issues.

To begin with, the company's orders were gradually dropping. Each time the company held a meeting, the marketing managers brought out a list of names, all of whom had been big customers of Zhenxing Leather Shoe Company in the past. Prior to the company going into trouble, customers would place orders every month but now these stopped coming in. Decreasing orders caused the factory machinery to stop, sending the workers into a panic. Although their panic was incomparable to that of Jiang Lina and Hu Weidong. Fewer orders meant less turnover; less turnover meant less profit. They were operating on very tight funds that seemed to be stretched even further.

Secondly, the company was failing to get back payments for goods that were in arrears. There were hundreds of customers in arrears for a total sum of RMB 200 million. These customers had either fled and hidden away, or were unconcerned by their debts, like dead pigs not fearing scalding water. Ai Mengya knew that they were not purposefully welshing on their debts. Rather, they were owed money by others, or else they were pressed themselves. They were in no position to settle their bill with Zhenxing Leather Shoe Company.

Thirdly, the company suffered from a lack of credibility. Too many customers had hit the road, and the company was operating very cautiously. New rules stipulated that customers were to pay for acquired goods on the spot. Similarly, suppliers also requested that the company pay for raw materials immediately. Jiang Lina had visited suppliers personally, hoping to reach an agreement to pay them monthly. They were all old connections made over the course of a decade, yet when they saw Jiang Lina, they all immediately complained. They claimed that those who owed them money were nowhere to be seen and that they were equally pressed by others to pay off their own debts. Otherwise, the suppliers said, they would have been more than willing to give Jiang Lina a helping hand in the face of hardship. Jiang Lina had already heard their excuses and still talked to them in vain. Suppliers no longer trusted Zhenxing Leather Shoe Company – they feared that it would go bust at any time.

The fourth issue was that the bank was in control of the company's money. Once the loan was paid off, Jiang Lina went to the head of the bank to renew it. He remained true to his word and sent a request to the higher-ups. Eventually, everything was checked and approved for a RMB hundred million loan – with a condition. The bank appointed someone to be a representative at the Zhenxing Leather Shoe Company. From then on, all inbound and outbound accounts were subject to the bank's review and monthly interest payments were deducted directly from the profits. In other words, the company's financial lifeline was in the bank's hands. Jiang Lina and Hu Weidong lacked any decision-making power and had no say in anything. Their hands were – quite simply – tied.

The fifth and final issue was that the RMB 300 million loan that Chen Naixing had had promised had yet yet to fully make it to the company. So far only RMB 180 million was paid as an advance, with another RMB 120 million still pending. Jiang Lina tried to press for the money several times. At first, Chen Naixing told her that he was collecting the money. Then he just stopped answering her phone calls altogether. Jiang Lina turned to Ai Mengya, who understood her concerns and called Chen Naixing. He merely replied that he did not have enough money on hand at the moment. His two large funds were placed with a couple of friends of his who were in business and had ultimately run away with his money. Ai Mengya reminded Chen Naixing of the five million that remained in the account of the Dongfang Guarantee Company and that could still be used. Chen Naixing said the five million made no difference to the total amount of RMB 120 million – it was better to keep that money exactly where it was. He needed it for other urgent matters anyway. The situation went far beyond Ai Mengya's imagination.

When she had agreed to Chen Naixing's request to become the chief financial officer at the Zhenxing Leather Shoe Company, all she knew was that many people had run away, and many businesses had been forced to close up shop. She had no idea these flights had exerted such a massive influence on Xinhe Street's economy. The Dongfang Guarantee Company's customer base was largely composed of young professionals. The company had hardly lost customers, and the only direct impact of the incidents on the company had been the decline in business volume. Therefore, she had been unable to assess the real impact of entrepreneurs running away. Only when she made it to the Zhenxing Leather Shoe Company was she truly at the epicentre of everything, and in that vortex she finally came to see the casualties left in the trail of it all. Chen Naixing himself had not escaped unscathed.

What Ai Mengya didn't know was that Chen Naixing's real problem was not the debt he owed to the Zhenxing Leather Shoe Company – it was Wang Wuxian. Wang Wuxian had already been captured by the police and spilt the beans on everything.

But hadn't he gone to the United States? He had indeed. He boarded the flight bound for America, and in America he had landed. He stayed in the United States for two months and then secretly returned to China. He was a lively man who enjoyed meeting with friends and having his little pets around. In the United States, he had no relatives, no friends. Even pet ownership in the US was subject to strict rules and regulations, giving legal protection to animals and making it harder to rescue them. Most importantly, Wang Wuxian could not speak a word of English. As soon as he made it to America, he was left mute. He could do nothing. Even so, he had promised Chen Naixing that he would stay in the United States, and that none of his information would fall in others' hands. As long as Wang Wuxian disappeared indefinitely, all evidence would be scattered to the wind. Finding a trace of Chen Naixing's involvement would be impossible. Wang Wuxian had really intended to stand by his promise. He took Chen Naixing's money and he had to pay the price. He ground his teeth and remained in the United States. In the end, it was Chen Naixing who failed to stand by his promise of sending him an additional two million dollars after the first month of his departure. At that point, Wang Wuxian called him, 'I thought you said you'd send me the rest of the money after a month?'

'I've had some trouble here,' said Chen Naixing over the phone.

'What kind of trouble?'

'Others have run away with my money too.'

'So you don't even have two million?' Wang Wuxian started to worry.

'I gave a large sum of money to the Zhenxing Leather Shoe Company. Wait for the business to work, and I'll give you the money.'

'How long will that take?'

'It'll be done in no time,' reassured Chen Naixing.

'How long is that?'

'Half a month, approximately.'

Wang Wuxian agreed. 'Fair enough! I'll wait half a month.'

'I warned you not to call me. Why didn't you stand by your word?'

'Look who's talking!'

Half a month later, Wang Wuxian called him again. 'How come I still don't have my money?'

'Something unforeseeable happened.'

'What is it?'

Chen Naixing decided to be blunt with him. 'The bank sent people to control the finances of the Zhenxing Leather Shoe Company. Right now I can't touch a cent.'

'So when the hell are you going to send me the money?'

'Wait a little longer! I'll give it to you as soon as possible.'

Ten more days went by, after which Wang Wuxian called Chen Naixing again. 'Why don't you keep your word?'

'It's not that I'm not keeping my word; the money is really blocked right now,' replied Chen Naixing again, impatiently.

'We had an agreement first.'

'I know. I still have a five million emergency fund here. If I can, I'll use it to transfer the money to you first,' reasoned Chen Naixing.

Wang Wuxian was also losing his patience and said to him, 'I am not a beggar waiting for you to cough up some money at your convenience. You must know everything I'm doing right now, I'm doing because of you.'

'I know, but right now I really have no money at hand.'

'Don't you have money in the States?'

'I do, but you know the law there. With such a large expenditure, I'd have the tax administration at my door immediately. You must wait for me to go to America.'

'And when's that going to happen?'

'Soon. As soon as I've handled all matters here.'

Wang Wuxian hung up the phone and decided that there was no point in waiting. He knew Chen Naixing was not deliberately defaulting on the two million. Chen Naixing obviously knew how important he was. Undoubtedly, he would have sent him the money had he had any. During his time in America, Wang Wuxian had not stopped paying attention to the dynamics of Xinhe Street. He knew that more and more people were running away every day, as though swept away by a typhoon; wherever one went, something was collapsing. Having been in charge of a guarantee company, he knew the current state of Xinhe Street. He thus came to a conclusion: Chen Naixing could no longer protect himself, nor was he in a position, any longer, to stand by his promises.

As for Chen Naixing's claim that he would give him the money once he landed in America, Wang Wuxian knew that those words were hollow, and merely a stratagem to get some breathing room. The sole aim of those words was to stabilise him. Chen Naixing wouldn't give him any money once he was in the States. Once he was here, Chen Naixing would be safe. Nobody would trace what he had done at Xinhe Street. Wang Wuxian's threats to him would cease to exist. Needless to say he would have no need to pay him a cent. Besides, once Chen Naixing made it to America, it would be virtually impossible to transfer two million his way for no apparent reason. Wang Wuxian was keenly aware of this.

Once he understood these two facts, he bought his plane ticket and returned to China.

Wisely, Wang Wuxian did not go back to Xinhe Street, where he knew the struggle was at its fiercest. Had he gone back, he'd be engulfed by the storm. Upon landing in Beijing, he made it to Shanghai by train, rented a place at a compound near Jing'an Temple, and withdrew from the outside world.

Once in Shanghai, Wang Wuxian got himself a fake ID card stating that his name was Wang Tianlai. He had started preparing this even before leaving Xinhe Street. Wang Tianlai was his cousin – a year younger and bearing some resemblance to Wang Wuxian. He died in a car accident five years ago. Wang Wuxian found his ID card while sorting out his stuff and kept it. Now it had come in handy.

Upon settling down in Shanghai, Wang Wuxian kept a low profile. He didn't try to find a job, but rather woke up bright and early in the morning to go exercise in the park, have breakfast outside, buy some daily necessities at the shops or supermarket, and get the morning newspaper on his way home. Once there, he read it without missing a single character – from the weather forecast to the obituaries. After lunch, he napped for an hour and a half, then woke up to surf the Internet. Sometimes he played some online games, and sometimes he read the news. In the evening, he usually sat down at some bar to have a glass of red wine and to chat with strangers. He then went back home before midnight.

In that quiet life of his, Wang Wuxian sometimes stumbled upon stray kittens and puppies that looked up at him with helpless eyes. Tears welled up in Wang Wuxian's eyes as soon as he cast his gaze upon them. He would immediately crouch and hug the poor little thing, saying in a baby voice, 'Come on, let's go home with Daddy.'

One month later, two police officers knocked at Wang Wuxian's door one afternoon. They showed him their credentials and informed him that neighbours reported that he was keeping a great deal of pets at home, and that this disturbed the neighbourhood at night. They were there to take a look.

Once the police officers were in, they asked to see his ID card. Wang Wuxian handed Wang Tianlai's card over to one of them while the other looked around and counted a total of three puppies and two kittens.

'Did you get them licenses?' One policeman asked.

'No, they're all stray animals. The poor things have nowhere to go.'

The police officer raised his eyebrows as he snapped a picture of the ID card. Wang Wuxian noticed this and his heart skipped a beat. The two police officers exchanged looks, and the one who was holding the ID card told Wang Wuxian, 'Take these pets and come with us!'

'What if I don't want to?'

'You don't have a choice. Come with us; we need to ask you a few questions. We are nice guys.'

Wang Wuxian had to put his pets in a cardboard box and follow the pair back to the police station. As soon as he got in and placed his cargo on the floor, he was handcuffed.

'What the hell do you have against me?' Wang Wuxian yelled.

No reply came. Instead, he was immediately taken to the interrogation room. One of the police officers took a few photos of him and went out. The one with the ID card asked, 'Who are you?'

'Why, I'm Wang Tianlai.'

'Wang Tianlai is deceased and his household registration was cancelled. Who the hell are you? Why are you assuming his identity? What for?'

'I really am Wang Tianlai.'

The police officer who had taken his picture quickly came back in and told his colleague, 'Results are back. His name is Wang Wuxian. He is colour-blind and pulled strings at Xinhe Street once to get his driving license. It was later revoked when he ran over someone.'

Wang Wuxian heard this and immediately hung his head. However, he was not too flustered. He knew he was but a mere pawn – Chen Naixing was the real king. If jail time was involved, Chen Naixing would be the first to wind up there.

On the night of Wang Wuxian's detention, Chen Naixing decided to flee to the United States. He ignored the fact that Wang Wuxian had returned to China, and he didn't know that he had been arrested in Shanghai. He just had a bad hunch. One month had gone by and Wang Wuxian had not nagged him about getting his money – that was out of character for him. Most importantly, however, Chen Naixing's entire invest-ment scheme had been involved in the loan-sharking scandal. Some companies that had done business with him were now gone, and those who remained were struggling. Originally, his greatest wish was to enter and gain control of the Zhenxing Leather Shoe Company, but now that he had attained his goal, he had reached a dead end. This made him feel somewhat disheartened and put him in a bit of a dilemma. He feared that if he persisted in his current line of business, Wang Wuxian would return. Wang Wuxian was a time bomb. In the the event that things went south, it would be difficult for him to get away. He mulled it all over and over, and eventually decided to go to the United States to lie low until everything blew over. His investments were all covert and would therefore not be affected by his leaving. Should the situation improve after a while, he would simply come back.

Chen Naixing called Ai Mengya prior to his departure. 'I am going to the United States,' he announced.

'When are you leaving?'

'Tomorrow. Please take care of all matters over at the Zhenxing Leather Shoe Company and the Dongfang Guarantee Company.'

'When are you coming back?' she asked.

'In a month, approximately. Call me if anything comes up, I'll pick up."

'Fine.'

After his call to Ai Mengya, Chen Naixing booked his ticket for the next day. Approximately half an hour later, someone knocked on his villa's door. He went to take a look and saw four armed police officers standing there, with two police cars behind them. The flash of the lightbars on top of the cars hurt Chen Naixing's eyes. He shut the doors and let out a sigh from his heart – the Wang Wuxian time bomb had undoubtedly exploded.

The following day, shortly after she made it to her office, Ai Mengya got a call from a police officer friend, 'Hey, you were colleagues with Chen Naixing back when you were working at the bank, right?'

'Yes!'

'Rumour has it that he was the backstage boss at the One Plus One Guarantee Company.'

'Where did you hear this rumour?'

'Both Wang Wuxian and he have been detained by the police. Wang Wuxian made a confession, saying that it was under Chen Naixing's instructions that he pulled Hu Weidong underwater. Apparently, the whole scheme was plotted by Chen Naixing.'

Ai Mengya did not say a word. She heard a loud banging sound in her mind, as if something huge had collapsed. Sitting in her office chair, her mind was blank. She did not know how long it took until she slowly stood up, sorted out her things in a matter-of-fact fashion, and left the Zhenxing Leather Shoe Company. Afterwards, she went to the Dongfang Guarantee Company and sat down at her office there. She wanted to do something, but she did not know what, exactly. It was noon already, but the thought of having a something to eat did not cross Ai Mengya's mind. She wanted to go out for a walk.

Not knowing where she wanted to go, she kept walking a few steps and stopping in the street, until she unexpectedly ended up at the entrance of the bank she had previously worked at. The location remained unchanged, except with an addition of a large new pavilion that was built after her time. She entered the building's lobby and took a look all around. She was looking for the credit department, but she couldn't find it. She did not ask anybody but sat quietly in the lobby, looking at people come and go. She knew nobody.

Upon exiting the lobby and going back onto the street, she resumed her slow walk until she got to the Audit Office. She did not go in. Instead, she stood outside for a long time, looking at it as if in a trance. She then turned back to look at pedestrians on the street – all of them in a hurry, all of them immersed in their own problems, nobody looking her way. Vehicles in the middle of the road lined up like ants moving a house, with the occasional angry honk of a horn sounding out.

By the time she made it back home, night had already fallen. As soon as Ai Mengya entered her place, she sat down on the floor, not wanting to stand up. She sat slumped over and quiet — so quiet she could hear her own heartbeat. Little by little, she regained some strength. Covering her face with her palms, she gently called out somebody's name and inevitably burst in tears.

The following day, she went back to the Dongfang Guarantee Company and transferred the five million deposited in the account.

That night, Ai Mengya boarded a flight bound to Canada.